KNOCK-KNOCK, WHO'S THERE?

Amber opened the tall door and leaned in to see if there was anything inside.

Suddenly something pushed her from behind. "Oww!" she cried as she landed hard on her knees. She heard the door to the wardrobe slam shut at her back.

She twisted herself around and pushed against the door. It didn't move at all. She felt around, but there was no handle on the inside. She pushed at the door again, and finally began pounding on it with both hands.

"Hey!" she yelled, hammering furiously. "Let me out of here! Help, somebody!"

Then she heard it. A faint rhythmic pulsing that grew stronger as she listened. It sounded like a heartbeat, only it wasn't Amber's. There was someone else in there with her. . . .

FOUL PLAY

HIDE-AND-SEEK

Based on an
original story

BY JOHN PEEL

PUFFIN BOOKS

PUFFIN BOOKS
Published by the Penguin Group
Penguin Books USA Inc., 375 Hudson Street, New York, New York 10014, U.S.A.
Penguin Books Ltd, 27 Wrights Lane, London W8 5TZ, England
Penguin Books Australia Ltd, Ringwood, Victoria, Australia
Penguin Books Canada Ltd, 10 Alcorn Avenue, Toronto, Ontario, Canada M4V 3B2
Penguin Books (N.Z.) Ltd, 182–190 Wairau Road, Auckland 10, New Zealand

Penguin Books Ltd, Registered Offices: Harmondsworth, Middlesex, England

First published in the United States of America by Puffin Books,
a division of Penguin Books USA Inc., 1993

1 3 5 7 9 10 8 6 4 2

LIBRARY OF CONGRESS CATALOGING-IN-PUBLICATION DATA
Peel, John, 1954–   Hide and seek / John Peel.
p.   cm.—(Foul play; 3) (Puffin high flyer)
Summary: After their school bus breaks down in a storm, a group of
children seeks shelter in an abandoned house where a game of hide-
and-seek might mean that you stay hidden forever.
ISBN 0-14-036054-9
[1. Supernatural—Fiction.   2. Mystery and detective stories.]
I. Title.   II. Series.   III. Series: Peel, John, 1954–   Foul play; 3.
PZ7.P348Hi   1993   [Fic]—dc20   92-37575

Printed in the United States of America
Set in Aster

High-Flyer™ is a trademark of Puffin Books, a division of Penguin Books USA Inc.

HIDE-AND-SEEK

Chapter One

WE ARE THE CHAMPIONS!

Rain hammered against the windshield as Alison Comer tried to make sense of the map. It didn't help that the flashlight she was using barely had any energy left in the batteries.

Beside her, Mr. Clarke, the gym teacher and coach of the swim team, was huddled over the wheel of the mini-van. "I hate thunderstorms," he muttered. Thunder rumbled so loudly Alison thought she could feel it shaking the van. "I especially hate driving in thunderstorms," he added.

A saw-toothed bolt of lightning stabbed across the blackness, and in its brief flash Alison tried again to figure out where they were. This morning she'd volunteered to be navigator. It was pointless, really, even trying to guess where they were. The Statue of Liberty could be standing there, ten feet off the road, and they'd never see it in this weather.

Three hours ago they'd beaten Lewton Junior High and

taken first place in the county trials. Now Heather and Amber were singing along with the boys in the minivan in an endless round of "A Hundred Bottles of Beer on the Wall." They were somewhere in the forties.

Amber Mangione and Heather Nowicki were sitting directly behind Alison. They were her best friends since the second grade.

Alison was tall, all arms and legs, with a mop of thick, tangled, dark brown hair. Amber was almost her exact opposite: she was short, a little overweight, with her blond hair cut chin-length and blunt. Heather was almost as tall as Alison, with long, jet-black hair. Alison still couldn't quite believe that they'd all been lucky enough to make the finals for the swim team.

The boys' team had also won their round. They were placed second overall in the county now. With three more meets to go, their chances looked good.

Brian Reed, Christopher Howard, and Matt Field were on the back seat of the van. The three of them were always competing—at anything and everything. Alison wasn't sure whether they were trying to see who could sing the loudest or just the worst. The song was getting on her nerves.

It must have been getting to Mr. Clarke too. "Will you please keep it down!" he yelled, irritably. The chorus died out, and a grumble of voices took its place.

Looking at the map again, Alison shook her head. "I haven't been able to pick out anything in this storm," she admitted. "Do you know where we are?"

"No," Mr. Clarke said wearily. "We may have missed

the turn. You'd think there would be a sign for *something* somewhere along this road!''

Alison knew what he meant. She'd been looking for anything that had a name on it to give them some clue as to where they were. But in this constant rain, all she could make out were vague shapes that were probably trees. It had been at least twenty minutes since they last saw a house.

Suddenly a flashing light appeared in the darkness. Mr. Clarke slammed on the brakes. The van screeched and skidded on the wet road, then came to a shaky halt. Though the rain washed everything into a blurry haze, it was impossible not to recognize the police car straddling the road ahead.

A policeman carrying a large flashlight and wearing a reflective plastic poncho stepped out of the gloom and tapped on the window. Mr. Clarke opened the window a crack. Rain sliced through the tiny opening, drenching him anyway.

''The bridge is out,'' the cop yelled over the noise of the thundering rain. ''You'll have to go the other way.''

''Bridge?'' Mr. Clarke echoed. ''What bridge? There isn't any bridge on Harlow Road.''

The cop shook his head. ''This isn't Harlow Road. You must have made a wrong turn about ten miles back. This is Route 17.''

Alison stared at the map and finally located Route 17 and the Paumanic River. They were *at least* ten miles from where they should have been. She felt herself burning with embarrassment. Some navigator she turned out to be!

Mr. Clarke gave a heavy sigh. "I guess we'd better turn back then. Ten miles, you say?"

"About that," the cop agreed. "But there's an easier way to get to Harlow." He used his flashlight beam to point. "Back about a mile there's a fork. Bear to the right. That's the old Mallon Road. Take that—oh, six, seven miles. That'll connect you with Harlow just outside of Miller's Ridge."

Mr. Clarke thanked the policeman and rolled up the window.

Shaking his head, he turned to Alison. "Okay, we'll turn around. Keep your eyes open for the fork in the road, okay?"

Still embarrassed, Alison said, "It's my fault we're not home, isn't it?"

"That's what you get for making a girl the navigator," jeered Matt from the back of the van. Matt Field, the tallest of the boys, had thick, dark hair and green eyes. Alison had to admit that he was really good-looking. He was also really mean.

"Tell me, Matt," Heather said in a bored voice. "Do you *always* have to be so obnoxious? I mean, were you born that way? Or is it like a disease you can't help?"

"That's enough," said Mr. Clarke firmly. "Alison's doing a good job in difficult conditions. But," he added, "it wouldn't hurt if you all kept an eye out for the fork, okay?"

Though this was a sensible request, it still hurt Alison. It was almost as if Mr. Clarke was saying that she couldn't be trusted to do her job properly. Matt laughed again, and she felt her cheeks flush.

Mr. Clarke didn't seem to notice any of this. He was concentrating on turning the vehicle around. A few minutes later they were heading back down the road they had just traveled. "Keep your eyes peeled," he warned them. "We're late enough as it is. Your parents are going to be worried."

"That's okay," Matt said. "Worrying is what they do. They're good at it."

"We need music," Brian decided. He struck a chord on an air guitar. "It's thrash night!"

"Drum solo!" Matt called, and started drumming frantically on the back of Heather's seat.

"Get your hands off—" Heather began.

"Calm down, please!" Mr. Clarke broke in. "Let's concentrate on finding this turnoff."

"There it is!" Alison said, pointing ahead of them. The headlights had picked out the fork in the road. She felt a little better for spotting it first.

Mr. Clarke nodded. "Right. We'll be home soon now." Carefully, he guided the van down the right-hand road. It seemed to dip downward, as if they were entering a tunnel burrowing into the earth. For all Alison could make out through the windows, they could even be doing that. The constant hammering of the rain washed out all the details of their surroundings.

In the back, Matt and Brian were having some kind of argument over which metal band was the most radical. Alison twisted around, trying to see what was happening. Brian had slipped out of his seat belt and was leaning over the back of the seat trying to dig his backpack out of the rear of the van. Matt was holding his legs and either

5

pretending or really trying to push him over the back of the seat into the pile of backpacks.

"Hey, dweeb, let go!" Brian yelled, swatting the air behind him with his free hand. This only made Matt push harder. Frustrated, Brian swung his bag over his shoulder, trying to hit his tormenter.

Then things happened very suddenly. The van hit a bump in the road. Brian lost his grip on his backpack. In mid-swing it sailed through the air, narrowly missing Heather to slam full force into the back of Mr. Clarke's neck.

Mr. Clarke let out a surprised yelp and jerked forward as the pack hit him. The next instant there was a scream of slipping tires. Alison's hands gripped the seat as the van skidded on the wet road. Terrified, she watched Mr. Clarke battle with the wheel, trying to keep the vehicle on the road.

"I hit the accelerator," he muttered, desperately punching his foot down on the brakes. But it was too late.

The van squealed across the road, and nosedived into blackness.

Chapter Two

EMERGENCY

Alison was slammed back into her seat and then flung forward as the van smashed into something. Her shoulder harness safely stopped her, but left an aching welt across her chest. There was the sound of metal tearing, and a horrible, shuddering clanging noise. Something hit the back of her head, leaving her stunned for a second. Someone was screaming.

For a long moment she was certain they were all going to die. The van was still moving. She could see the shock and fear on Mr. Clarke's face as he realized he couldn't control the vehicle. A tree appeared out of the gloom ahead of them. It was like a slow-motion horror movie. The van hit the tree, causing a side window to explode in a shower of glass and rain. One sliver grazed Alison's cheek like a razor. She could feel the blood starting to flow. Another chunk shot into the seat back, inches from her throat. A few more inches and she'd have been killed.

Alison barely caught her breath from this narrow

escape when the front of the van pitched sharply downward and the lights went dead. The van fell, hitting the ground on one wheel with a jarring thud that shook every bone in Alison's body. Then, with a hollow grating sound, the van collapsed onto its side.

She was still alive. She was sure of that, because her cheek burned where the glass had cut her. She wiped at it with a corner of her T-shirt. She was bleeding, but not too badly.

It felt odd hanging in the air by her seat belt. Underneath her now, instead of next to her, Mr. Clarke groaned.

Other sounds began to sort themselves out as Alison's head stopped spinning. One of the boys was moaning. Amber's breath was coming in short, heavy pants, like she was about to start sobbing uncontrollably.

"Is everyone okay?" asked Mr. Clarke. There was a clicking sound as he unfastened his seat belt. Then he struggled around to a crouching position on the wreckage of the door.

"I'm okay," Alison managed to tell him.

"Good," he said. He reached up to her. "Okay, release your belt, and I'll help you to stand."

She nodded and opened the buckle, and Mr. Clarke helped her get her footing beside him. She felt faint, but fought down the giddiness and looked over the rest of the van.

It was a real mess. Everything had been thrown about in the crash. Two windows had shattered. Rain was showering over them all. Alison blinked as she realized that she was soaked. Somehow she simply hadn't noticed before.

Amber was a soggy mess on the seat. She'd slipped partially out of her belt and was struggling to sit upright and get the belt off. Mr. Clarke went to help her while Alison went to Heather, who was bent over in her seat, gasping for breath. "Are you okay?" Alison asked.

Heather nodded, but rubbed at her leg. Alison saw a thin line of blood near the hem of her shorts. "You caught some glass too," she said.

"It's not bad," Heather said bravely. "What about the others?"

There was movement from the backseat. Chris and Matt were both freeing themselves from the pile of bags that had fallen on them.

Chris's face looked terribly thin and frightened. "Brian's out cold," he said. "And his leg looks kind of funny. Something's wrong with it."

Alison remembered what had been happening. Brian had been looking for his bag, and he hadn't had his seat belt fastened. When the van had crashed, he must have fallen.

Mr. Clarke shuffled past Alison and headed for the back of the van to examine Brian. Meanwhile, Amber was breathing in short, frightened jerks.

"It's okay," Heather told her, putting an arm around her. "We're okay."

"I'm . . . I'm all right." Amber's voice was shaking. "I was just so scared."

"Me, too," Alison admitted. She glanced at the back of

the van. Mr. Clarke had managed to get the unconscious Brian out of the tangled metal and slashed seats.

"Is he going to be okay?" Chris asked.

"I think his leg is broken," Mr. Clarke replied grimly. He glanced around the shattered van. "There's a long metal box under the front seat. It's a first-aid kit. Can one of you bring it to me?"

Alison got the first-aid kit, and Mr. Clarke splinted Brian's leg. Together, Alison and Chris managed to see to the minor cuts and bruises that the rest of them had suffered.

Brian came to and sat up as Mr. Clarke finished working on him. "Take it easy," the teacher said. "Are you in pain?"

Brian flexed his foot and winced. "Only if I try to move."

"Then don't," Mr. Clarke told him.

"What are we going to do now?" asked Amber in a quavery voice. She sounded every bit as scared as Alison felt.

"I'm going to get help," Mr. Clarke told them. "In his condition, I don't think Brian should be moved." He scratched at his chin. "I'm going to try to get back to the policeman we saw," he said finally. "You'd all better stay here with the van. Look out for cars and wave them down if you see any. But be careful. They might not see you until the last second in this weather."

"We'll be lucky if another car comes along," muttered Matt. "Except for that cop, we haven't seen another sign of civilization for *hours*."

"Maybe you could put something over the broken windows to keep the rain out," Mr. Clarke went on. "It may take me a while to get back to the bridge in this weather. Try not to get too worried while you wait."

He reached up to the door, which was now over his head. With some effort, he managed to get it to creak open. Then he hoisted himself out of the van. The van shook as he settled on the outside for a moment. "I'll be as quick as I can," he promised. He slammed the door shut, then jumped off and vanished into the darkness of the storm.

Alison looked at her friends. Amber was pale but trying to stay brave. Heather gave her a shaky half grin. Matt had a sour expression on his face—guilt or anger? Chris was nervously biting his lower lip. Brian looked tired and in pain.

What would they do now?

"Maybe we should cover over the windows," Alison suggested.

"We can't get much wetter than we already are," grumbled Matt. But he joined the rest of them in getting towels from their gym bags and trying to tie them over the broken windows.

"Wait a minute," Heather said. She sniffed loudly. "Do you smell something?"

Alison stopped and took a sniff herself. "Gas," she whispered.

"The tank must have been punctured in the crash!" Chris said. "The van's going to blow up!"

"I don't think so," Heather said. "You need a spark or something for that."

"You want to wait around just in case?" asked Matt.

He jumped for the door. "I'm getting out of this death trap."

Matt wrenched the door open with a furious pull. Then, grunting, he pulled himself out onto the top of the wreck. He was about to jump down when Chris called out angrily, "Wait a minute and help us out!"

For a moment, Matt looked like he was going to refuse. Then he nodded, kneeling at the edge of the gap. "Come on, move it," he said, holding down a hand. Heather grabbed it, and scrambled up beside him. Amber looked at the others uncertainly.

"Go on," Alison told her. "You next."

She grabbed Matt and Heather's offered hands and clambered up. Alison turned to look at Brian.

"Think you can make it?" she asked.

"I'll try," he said. "I'm not staying here, that's for sure." Chris helped him stand up on his good leg. Alison grabbed his other arm. Trying to pretend she couldn't see the pain in Brian's eyes, she helped Chris half walk, half drag him to the doorway.

Eager hands reached down. Brian stretched to meet them. Once Brian had a tight grip, Chris let go of him and grabbed Brian's good leg. With difficulty, pushing and pulling, the five of them managed to get Brian out of the van.

A few minutes later all six of them were standing outside the van. Rain was still sweeping across the sky.

"Great," muttered Matt. "We're in the middle of nowhere, no sign of shelter anywhere, we're totally drenched, and it's still pouring down."

"I think I was drier during the swim meet," Chris agreed. His long blond hair was plastered flat against his head, and rain was dripping into his eyes. He looked at Brian, whose eyes were squeezed tight against the pain. "If you lean on me and Matt, do you think you can walk?"

Brian nodded and put one arm on each of their shoulders. Slowly, he began to limp away from the wrecked van. The three girls followed, staying close.

A few minutes later Alison turned around. The van was gone, lost in the gloom behind them.

Amber noticed her staring. "Alison," she said nervously, "I don't see the van anymore. What if we can't find it again?"

"Don't worry. It can't go anywhere," Alison assured her. "We'll find it." But the words felt like a lie. Some part of her was sure that the van had been swallowed by the storm. And some part of her was sure they'd never see it again.

ANYONE HOME?

Alison felt as if they'd been walking for hours. The storm hadn't let up at all. Rain whipped around them, and the thunder was crashing so loudly she almost expected the earth to shake. Like the rest of them, she was cold and wet and miserable. And completely lost.

"Where are we going?" Heather asked, shouting to be heard over the storm.

Matt pointed off into the darkness. "There are some trees over there that we can use for shelter."

"Isn't that dangerous?" Amber asked. "I mean, doesn't lightning hit trees?" As if to underline Amber's question, a blaze of jagged lightning lit the sky.

"Yeah," Chris agreed. "But if we stay out here, we'll probably drown."

Brian sneezed. "I think I've already got pneumonia."

"And you can't go much farther on your leg," Alison said. She was worried. There were no houses in sight, and Brian looked terrible.

"Oh, I'm okay," he said, but the tremor in his voice betrayed him.

14

"Look," Heather yelled, pointing off to the west as another slash of lightning illuminated the gloom. Alison followed her friend's pointing finger and stared in amazement.

Atop a nearby slope stood a large house. It was dark against the sky for a second, and then she could make out lights in the windows.

"Why didn't we see that when we were driving?" Alison asked, astonished.

"Who cares?" Matt replied. "Let's get up there and out of the rain!"

As they drew closer, Alison could make out the shape of the house. It was large and squarish, with dozens of windows. Four huge wooden pillars held up a large balcony over the main door. The place was definitely old, Alison decided, maybe even hundreds of years old.

Amber grabbed the huge iron ring on the door and began knocking. Even over the roar of the storm, Alison could hear the hollow echo inside the house.

No one answered.

"Maybe no one's home," Heather said. "Or maybe they didn't hear us."

Amber tried again. And again there was no answer.

"Forget it, Amber," Matt said impatiently. "There's no one home, and I'm not staying outside in the rain."

Alison looked at him in disbelief. "You're not talking about breaking in?"

Matt shrugged. "If nobody's home, then we might as well be drying out inside."

Heather stared unhappily at the door. "What if there's a burglar alarm?"

"All the better," Matt said, grinning. "Then the cops will come and get us, and we can get home. We've even got a good excuse." He pointed at Brian. "We were looking for help for our injured friend. And, anyway," he added, "there's probably a phone inside. We could call for help." He looked at the other five. "So you coming with me? Or do you want to stay out here and get pneumonia?"

"I guess we're with you," Amber said reluctantly.

Matt frowned at the door for a moment. "Might as well start with the door knob," he said. He stepped forward and turned the knob. The heavy, wooden door swung open effortlessly. "I think this is our invite," he said, grinning.

The others followed him inside. They came to a stop in the hallway, looking around in silent amazement. High-ceilinged rooms opened on either side of the hall. Directly in front of them was a large stairway of polished wood, leading to the upper floor of the house. Immense carved banisters lined both sides of the stairs. On the second floor a balcony edged the inside of the great hall and led to what looked like two long corridors.

"Hello!" Matt yelled loudly. "Anyone home? Hello?" His voice echoed through the hall, but there was no reply. "Maybe they got stuck in the storm or something."

"This house is so big, they probably didn't hear us," Chris said.

"What a place," Amber said softly. "Look at that chandelier. I've never seen one lit with candles before."

Alison followed Amber's gaze and saw a great crystal

chandelier and dozens of brightly burning white candles. Then Brian gave a low moan, and she forgot about the decor. They had to get him help fast. "Let's look for a phone," she said. "And while we're at it, we can try to find the people who live here and maybe some towels. I'm sure whoever lives here won't want us dripping all over their floors."

"Right," agreed Matt. "Chris, you stay here with Brian. Heather, you and Amber look on this floor. Alison, you and I can check upstairs."

"Who made you boss?" Heather demanded.

"Let's not argue about it," Alison said quickly.

She started up the stairs, and Matt trailed behind her, stomping loudly and beating a rhythm out on the banister. "What are you trying to do?" she demanded. "Wake the dead?"

Matt nodded. "If there's someone upstairs, I want them to know we're coming. That way we won't give some old lady a heart attack if we just appear in front of her."

Alison didn't like this idea much. Something about the dignified old house made her feel that it wasn't used to a lot of noise. And she had the oddest feeling—that somehow Matt's clattering was disturbing something that had been still for a very long time.

At the top of the stairs they paused. Two corridors led off to the left and right. "Take your pick," Matt said.

"I'll go to the right," Alison decided, heading toward the nearest door. She tapped on it, and when there was no reply, she pushed it open.

17

It led to a small bedroom. A low wooden dresser with beautifully carved flowers was tucked beneath the window. Across from it was a straight-backed chair with a cane seat. Then a bed, neatly made and turned down, as if waiting for someone to hop in. A small table beside the bed held a book and a single lit candle in a wooden stand. The only other item of furniture in the room was a large pine wardrobe.

Alison thought about taking the quilt off the bed, then hesitated. Something about disturbing this room seemed wrong. She closed the door again. "Nothing useful here," she reported.

Matt had gone the other way. "An empty bedroom," he called out, going to another door. Alison nodded, and went to the next door on her side.

This led into what was obviously a bathroom of sorts, but not like any bathroom she'd ever seen. There was no sink or toilet. A large folding screen stood in the center of the room. It was painted with a landscape of rolling hills. Behind the screen was a very large metal tub. One end was taller than the other, and beside it on a small table lay a long-handled brush and a large cake of soap. There were no taps, and there was no sign of a way to get water into the room. A very weird bathroom, Alison decided.

She was about to leave when she noticed a chair by the window. On it was a thick, fluffy pile of green towels.

Sticking her head back out the door, Alison yelled for Matt. He stared into the room, his green eyes questioning. "What's this supposed to be?"

"A bathroom. Sort of. At least they have towels," Alison replied.

"If only finding a phone were this easy," Matt said. "I didn't see one anywhere, did you?"

Alison shook her head. It was kind of weird, she thought. In her own house, there were five phones—two upstairs, two down, and one even in the basement. "I guess the people who live here are kind of old-fashioned," she told Matt with a shrug.

She and Matt each picked up a stack of towels and then headed downstairs, calling for Heather and Amber to join them.

Back in the hallway, Alison handed towels to Chris and Brian, then began to dry her own hair.

Heather and Amber appeared a few minutes later.

"Guess what we found?" said Amber.

"A telephone?" Alison asked hopefully.

"Nothing like that," Heather replied. "But there's a room with some big, comfortable chairs and a great fire going in the fireplace. Brian can rest, and we can all warm up."

"Let's go," Brian said. His teeth were chattering and his face was much paler than usual. He was obviously in pain.

Heather led the way into the room she'd described. It was a study, Alison decided. Two of the walls were covered floor to ceiling with bookshelves. A third wall framed two tall windows with dark red curtains. And the fourth wall framed the blazing fireplace.

Chris helped Brian into one of the wing-backed chairs in front of the fire. His splinted leg was propped on a low footstool. Alison sat down across from him, watching as he shut his eyes and took deep even breaths. She knew

19

what he was doing—trying to control the pain. "Are you all right?" she asked.

He nodded. "Fine." He opened his eyes. "Are you all going to stand around and watch me?"

Chris, who was Brian's best friend, went over to the shelves. "All these books have leather bindings," he said in surprise.

"Any good slasher stories?" Matt asked.

"Only if you think *A Guide to Commonly Observed New Hampshire Birds* is scary. Looks like they're all like that—nature guides and science books."

"No one found a phone?" Brian asked.

Amber shook her head. "I don't even think this place has electricity. This floor, at least, is all lit with candles."

"So is the second," Alison said. "And there was no running water in the bathroom." Suddenly Alison's skin felt cold. Maybe it was just from being wet, but . . . "If there's nobody here," she said slowly, "then who lit the candles and made this fire?"

"Who knows?" Matt didn't sound too concerned. "Maybe they're hiding from us for some reason. Maybe they're wacko and hate visitors. You know, like those people who can't ever leave their houses, 'cause they're afraid of open spaces." Then he grinned wickedly. "Or maybe they're psychopaths, hiding and waiting till we go to sleep, so they can creep out and cut our throats."

Amber shivered. "Don't even *joke* about it."

"Who's joking?" asked Matt. "They *could* be waiting to make human sacrifices out of us."

"Cut it out, Matt," Alison said. "Stop trying to scare people, okay?"

"Wimps."

"Stop it," said Heather. She was sitting by the fire, toweling off her long hair. "There *is* something weird about this house. This whole night's been strange." She looked up at Brian. "And you're still shivering. Isn't the fire helping?"

Brian wasn't just shivering, Alison realized. He was shaking violently. And she knew why. "It's because you're still wearing that heavy cotton sweater," she told him. "It'll take forever to dry, even sitting in front of the fire."

"Look," Matt said restlessly. "There are dozens of bedrooms upstairs. We'll go find you some dry clothes."

"Or we can bring down a blanket," Alison said.

Brian looked like he was about to protest, but Chris said, "They're right. Here." He handed him two towels. "You can wrap up in these for now."

Matt was already moving toward the door. "Come on," he said. "We've got a mission now: to find something that fits Brian. We can split up again." He smiled at Heather. "Okay if I suggest that, or do you want to give the orders this time?"

Heather looked uncomfortable. "I don't like borrowing things without asking."

Matt spread his arms. "Who is there to ask?"

"That's the problem," Amber said nervously. "We may be in this house with someone we haven't seen."

Matt ignored her and turned to Chris. "You stay here with Brian. We'll be back soon."

Alison felt very strange as she headed back upstairs. Matt's joke about psychopaths wouldn't leave her head.

This *was* a spooky old house, and she had a lot of questions. Where were the owners of the house? Why didn't they have electricity or running water? Was there someone in the house, hiding from them? Waiting for them?

She just wondered whether she'd be happier to find the answers or to never know at all.

At the top of the stairs Matt took charge. Again. "Okay, Heather, you start down at the end of the corridor on the left. Amber, you try the rooms at the very end on the right. I'll go into the ones I saw before, and Alison will check out the ones she was in."

"Yes, Your Highness," Heather said with a mock bow.

"Your word is our command," Amber added with a giggle.

Matt scowled at them, then at Alison. "What's *your* problem?"

"You're so bossy," she told him.

"At least I'm coming up with plans." Matt turned toward the room he was going to search. "If you have a better idea, go with it."

Alison sighed and turned toward the rooms she'd been in. I'll start with the small bedroom, she thought. It was the first room on the right, and she remembered seeing a wardrobe in there.

She opened the wooden door and stopped, unable to believe what she was seeing. The room with the neatly turned-down bed and the dresser and the wardrobe was gone. In its place was a solid brick wall.

Chapter Four

ALONE IN THE STUDY

Chris stood in the doorway of the study, hoping the others would be quick. There was something about this house that scared him. He sat down across from Brian in the other wing-backed chair. "Some furniture, huh?" he said, mostly to make conversation.

"Yeah," Brian answered with a shiver. "Do you think you could help me move this chair closer to the fire?"

Chris frowned. "You're pretty close as it is. If I move you any closer, you'll be toast."

Brian pulled the towels more tightly around his shoulders. His entire body was shaking. And although just a little while ago he'd been terribly pale, now his face was flushed.

"Are you running a fever?" Chris asked.

Brian nodded. "I think so. My leg hurts like crazy, and I don't feel so good."

Chris stood up uneasily. "We've got to get you a

doctor. Maybe I should go out, see if there are any neighbors.''

''No!'' Brian said. ''I mean, I don't really want to be down here on my own. And don't tell the others I'm sick. Matt will call me a wimp or a crybaby.''

''Forget Matt!'' Chris told him. ''He's just a bully who—''

A high-pitched scream tore through the house.

''That sounded like Alison,'' Brian said.

Chris nodded. ''Will you be all right if I leave you for a few minutes?''

''I guess,'' Brian said, but Chris was already on his way out of the study.

A moment later he found Alison near the top of the stairs. Matt, Heather, and Amber were with her. ''What happened?'' Chris asked.

''Alison's imagining things,'' Matt replied.

''I am *not* imagining things,'' Alison argued. She pointed to the door on the right that was nearest to the stairs. ''When we were up here before, I went through that door. Inside was a little bedroom with this small wooden dresser that had flowers carved into it. There was a table by the bed that had a book and a candle on it. And there was a wardrobe. And I just opened the door again, and there was a solid brick wall.''

''Sure, Alison,'' Matt jeered. ''Whatever you say.'' He walked up to the door and opened it.

Chris peered into the room. ''What's the problem? That's exactly the room Alison described.''

Alison turned a sick shade of green. ''It wasn't here a

24

minute ago," she insisted. "I opened that same door and saw a brick wall." She sat down and rested her head on her knees. "I must be losing my mind."

"What did you see?" Chris asked Heather and Amber.

"We just got here," Heather answered. "So we're seeing it for the first time, just like you. But this house is kind of weird."

"Listen," Matt said. "Just because Alison is seeing things is no reason for everyone to get freaked."

"Shut up, Matt," Alison muttered.

Chris walked into the room and opened the wardrobe. "Empty," he reported. "Do you guys want to keep searching? Or—"

"I'll be fine," Alison said, standing up.

"When you get glasses," Matt added.

"Great," said Chris impatiently. "Then I'd better get back down to Brian. He's not doing so well."

Brian sat in the chair by the fire, trying to stay awake. He was still shivering with cold, and yet beads of sweat were dripping down his forehead. He was definitely feverish. And his leg hurt.

He tried to focus his attention on the old oak mantel above the fireplace. The strange carvings showed people dressed in the clothes of some earlier century. The women wore long dresses, and the men wore jackets with long tails. They kept dancing in and out of focus. He rubbed his eyes, but it didn't help.

This was all Matt's fault. Brian had never liked Matt. He was a bully—mean, sarcastic, never happy unless everyone else was doing things his way. It was Matt who tried to push him over the edge of the seat. If it hadn't been for Matt, Brian never would have thrown his pack. The van never would have crashed. And he wouldn't be sitting here now with a broken leg, burning up with fever.

His mind was drifting slightly, hovering between fevered sleep and wakefulness. His head jerked forward. For a second Brian blacked out.

Then he snapped back awake. The flames in the fireplace had grown dim. And the chair that Chris had been sitting in was skittering back and forth across the floor. *Are we in the middle of an earthquake?* Brian asked himself foggily.

Everything else in the room was still.

Brian closed his eyes and opened them again. The chair was still moving, caught in some crazy dance. He looked around the room for Chris, desperately wanting someone to tell him that he wasn't imagining this. The study was empty. Chris must still be with the others. *What happened to Alison?* he wondered.

When the chair began to move in circles, Brian decided he'd had enough. He struggled to get to his feet, but his leg was throbbing. The tiniest movement sent pain streaking through his entire body.

He heard the sound of a door slamming. "Chris?" he tried to shout, but his voice was so weak that he knew no one could hear him.

Brian watched amazed as the chair returned to its place, just a foot away from him.

"I *was* imagining things," he said.

Then, on one of the shelves a wooden box opened and a brown cigar floated out. Brian blinked his eyes as the tip of the cigar hovered over the fire, lighting itself. The cigar then floated over to the side of the empty chair and remained there—as if some invisible person sat in the chair smoking it.

"This is too strange," Brian said aloud. "I'm out of here now!" But when he tried to stand, the pain was so bad he nearly fainted. He sank back into the chair, panting.

"Help!" he called out. "Someone help me!"

There was a small end table next to the chair. As Brian watched, terrified, a drawer in it opened and a round metal ashtray floated to the top of the table. The drawer closed. The cigar settled itself in the ashtray.

I'm sitting here with a ghost, Brian thought wildly. *A ghost who smokes cigars. Who knows? Maybe he's friendly.*

And then Brian realized that he wasn't. The cigar rose from the ashtray, hovered a minute, and then floated toward Brian.

The glowing red end floated closer and closer. It was coming straight for his face. He could feel its heat on his skin. Brian ducked his head to the side. The cigar moved with him.

And Brian shut his eyes and screamed until his throat was raw.

"Scaredy-cat!" jeered a familiar voice.

Brian opened his eyes and found himself staring up into Matt's sneering face. The cigar was gone. "It can't hurt you," Matt said. "It's just a shadow from the past." Then he leaned forward, eyes glittering in the light of the fire. "But *I* can hurt you, you miserable little wimp. I'm the one you ought to be frightened of." Then Matt reached up with his hand. Gripping his own hair, he suddenly jerked his hand forward and down.

His entire face peeled away like a mask. Beneath it a white skull glistened in the light from the fire.

Matt bent forward, his white skull-face looming over Brian. "I'm going to get you," he promised. "And when I do, it's going to be much worse than this." Then he threw his skull-head back and laughed and laughed and laughed.

MORE
QUESTIONS

Alison and Heather walked into the larger of the two
bedrooms that Alison had found before. Defying Matt's
orders, they'd decided to search together.

"That's odd," Alison said.

"What is?"

Alison pointed to an old-fashioned green velvet dress
that was lying across the bed. "That wasn't here when I
was in this room before." The dress was trimmed with
cream-colored lace and had tiny pearl buttons up the
front. Alison picked it up and held it against herself. It was
exactly her size, but the skirt went all the way to the floor.
"What do you think?" she asked her friend.

Heather wrinkled her nose. "It's okay if you want to
dress for Halloween." She crossed the room and opened
the wardrobe, muttering, "How come this place doesn't
have normal closets?" She pulled out a second dress
made of stiff blue wool and gave her opinion of it in one
word: "Yuk!"

Alison grinned at her friend. "You're so picky!"

Heather shrugged. "Excuse me if I don't feel like dressing like someone out of an old movie—a *really* old movie."

"I don't think these are costumes," Alison said. "I think these dresses are the real thing. They're vintage, probably valuable antiques."

Heather shrugged as she held out a third and then a fourth dress. These were adult-size but cut in the same funny style. "You're probably right. I just can't imagine actually wearing things like this. How's anyone supposed to breathe with such tight, little waists? Give me jeans and a T-shirt any day!"

"I know how you feel," Alison replied. Pretty as the green dress was, she had no desire to wear it. It felt like the dress was made for a very different type of person. She crossed to the dresser and opened the top drawer. It was filled with pairs of thick, white stockings and a few black ones. "Weird." She opened the next drawer and began to laugh. "Heather, you've got to see this!" She held up a pair of the largest, baggiest underpants she'd ever seen. "I think these are what they used to call drawers."

"You know what's strange about them?" Heather said. "I think they were made for someone your size. You want to try them on?"

"No," Alison said firmly. "Let's try another room. Maybe we'll find some better stuff."

They skipped the bathroom, since Alison knew there was nothing in there. The next room was a much larger bedroom. Alison thought it was one of the most elegant rooms she'd ever seen. A deep red oriental carpet covered the floor. The bed was a huge four-poster with rich ivory curtains hanging from the posts. A thick feather comforter lay across the bed.

The walls were covered with old-fashioned paintings. There were hunting scenes and landscapes that reminded Alison of things she'd seen in museums. There was a bookcase filled with expensive-looking leather-bound books. There was also a small antique desk. Alison went over to examine it more closely. Its top held a neat arrangement of old-fashioned writing tools: a small inkpot—Alison lifted the lid and saw real ink—and two polished wooden pens with glistening nibs.

"This is wild," Heather whispered. "It's so ancient."

"The whole house is," Alison said thoughtfully. "It's like nothing has changed since the last century."

Heather reached for a strand of her hair and began to braid it. That was always what she did when she was trying to figure something out. "Maybe this place is a museum," she suggested. "It can't be a regular house. I mean, who'd actually want to live here without things like a phone or a television?"

Alison took a quick look inside the wardrobe. "I don't think we're going to find anything to fit Brian in here," she said. "Let's try another room."

Back in the corridor, Alison pulled the next door open. It was a walk-in closet of some kind, not really a room. Wooden shelves lined one wall from top to bottom, but were all bare. Shrugging, Alison closed the door. "Not in use, I guess.'' She went to the next door, which opened into a small workroom. There was an old-fashioned sewing basket there, and a dressmaker's stand that looked vaguely like a woman's body. On the stand was a dress, which looked like it was being edged with lace. Like the other dresses they'd seen, it reached down to the floor.

''I guess that proves it,'' Heather said, sighing theatrically. ''It's grandma's old dresses or nothing for us. I think I'll just stand in front of the fire.''

''Me too,'' Alison agreed.

''Hey, you two!'' Heather yelled to Matt and Amber. ''Did you find anything?''

Matt popped out of a door down the other corridor. ''Did we ever!'' he said. ''You won't believe this stuff!''

Alison and Heather looked at each other and shrugged, then went to join Matt and Amber. This was clearly a boy's room, Alison saw. There was a twin bed with a big wooden chest at its foot. A patchwork quilt was neatly folded on top of the chest. A small brass telescope rested on a sturdy table next to the window. Several books were stacked next to the telescope, and a sheet of paper with scraggly writing on it stuck out from the bottom book.

Alison pulled out the paper. The writing was hard to read, but it seemed to be a record of different constellations observed through the telescope. The date on it shook her. ''Look at this!'' she said, ''April 25, 1864.''

''Today is April twenty-fifth,'' Heather pointed out.

''So what?'' Amber asked.

Amber was rooting about in a larger trunk that stood

opposite the window. She pulled out trousers, shirts, and sweaters. "These clothes are not exactly cool," she said, frowning.

"They're better than what we found," Heather assured her.

But Alison was no longer worried about clothing. There was something eerie about being in this house on April 25 and finding notes made on the same date over a hundred years ago. It almost felt as if there were a connection— between Alison and her friends and whoever had lived here in the year 1864.

"What I don't get," she said aloud, "is what went on between the 1860s and the 1990s. This place looks like nothing in it has changed in a hundred years or more. Why?"

"Maybe nothing has," said Matt. "Maybe it's some freaky old museum."

"If this house really were a museum," Alison went on, "we would have seen a place where they took money or sold postcards or something. Wouldn't we?"

"Maybe, maybe not." Heather mused.

"So it's not a museum." Matt sounded bored. "Just chill out," he advised. "Let's get some of this warm stuff down to Brian. Remember, we're only here as long as the storm lasts."

"I hope so," Alison said slowly. But too many things didn't make sense. The whole house _felt_ wrong. No one seemed to live here, and yet someone had lit a fire. And someone had left out a dress for a girl exactly her size.

_____

Chris sat in the study in the chair across from Brian, watching his friend sleep. He'd been sleeping ever since Chris returned from the second floor. He could tell Brian was still feverish. His face was flushed, and he was nodding restlessly, moaning and muttering.

A few feet from them the fire crackled, warm and comforting. Chris almost found himself dozing off. He probably would have if Brian hadn't sat bolt upright and begun screaming. It was a bloodchilling sound that went on and on as if he'd never stop. As if he couldn't stop.

Chris was by his side at once. "Brian, calm down. It's me, Chris. Everything's okay. Everything's fine."

Finally Brian seemed to snap out of it. The awful screaming stopped, and his eyes fluttered open.

Chris looked down at him, concerned. "Hey, Bri, it's okay," he soothed him. "You were just having some kind of nightmare, buddy."

Brian shook his head. His eyes were open wide, and he was staring at a spot across the room. "Matt was in here. He stood where you're standing now, and he threatened me. He—"

"Matt's still upstairs," Chris said soothingly. "Now tell me what happened."

Slowly Brian told him about the dancing chair and the ghostly cigar. Finally, he told him about Matt, and how Matt somehow tore his face off to reveal the skull beneath it. "He's not like you and me. He's evil, Chris. And we're trapped in this house with him."

Chris eyed his friend with concern. "Don't you think you're going a little overboard? I mean, Matt *is* a pain and all, but—"

"He's evil," Brian insisted. "He's after me. He's going to get me."

Chris sat back in the other chair. "It's not that I don't believe you. I mean, I don't think you're lying or anything. But this chair *looks* like it hasn't moved, and I don't see any cigars or ashtrays or skulls. Sounds like a bad fever dream to me."

Brian shook his head. "It was all real."

"Alison saw something weird, too," Chris admitted. "Though not *this* weird."

"I'm not making this up," Brian said stubbornly. "The box of cigars is on that shelf there. See if one cigar is missing."

Chris gave him a doubtful glance but got the cigar box down and brought it over to Brian.

Brian opened the box. "It's empty," he said in disbelief.

Chris said nothing.

"You don't believe me," Brian said.

Chris sighed and ran a hand through his long blond hair. "I believe you had a fever dream," he said. He walked over to the window and peered through the dark red curtain. "This storm's got to break soon. Try and get some rest. I promise we'll get you help."

"Thanks a lot," Brian muttered, but his eyes were drifting closed again.

Chris shrugged and stared out the window. *Did I just lie?* he wondered. *Is this storm ever going to break?* Lightning still streaked the sky, and rain was still lashing at the house.

What if they couldn't get help for Brian? He and Brian

35

had been friends since third grade. Matt had transferred into their class two years later. He'd always given Brian a hard time, but Brian had never sounded so scared of Matt before. Today at the swim meet Brian had gotten off to a slow start in the team medley, and Matt had needled him about it the whole time they were in the locker room. Had Matt threatened him? Chris wondered.

He wondered if he should tell the others what Brian had seen. No, he decided. Matt would just make fun of Brian, and the others would be upset. Besides, it was only a fever dream.

But as he stared out into the rain Brian's words played over and over in his mind. *"He's not like you and me. He's evil, Chris. And we're trapped in this house with him."*

HIDE . . .

Heather woke Brian again when they all came downstairs with the spare clothes they'd scavenged. Brian put on a thick brown sweater that was nearly the same color as his hair. Alison had insisted on also tucking a comforter over his legs. Brian had barely said a word and now he'd fallen back asleep.

The other members of the swim team gathered around the fire. They were all bored and restless and edgy. Outside the rain was still coming down in sheets.

"I wonder where Mr. Clarke is," Amber said in a worried tone.

Heather stood up and stretched. "It's Brian I'm worried about. He should be in a hospital."

"I know," Chris agreed. Normally the calmest one of them all, he looked ready to crack. "I'm sick of just sitting here, waiting," he blurted.

"There's not much else to do," Matt grumbled. "The

books are boring—unless you're into bird watching. There's no TV, no CD player, no VCR—''

"We could play a game," Amber suggested.

"There *aren't* any games," Matt retorted.

"Well, let's make one up," Chris said, sounding desperate.

Matt glanced around him. "How about hide-and-seek?"

"Isn't that a little young?" Heather asked sarcastically.

"Does it matter?" Matt retorted. "Anything's got to be better than just sitting here."

He had a point, Heather realized. The longer they sat, the more she worried. Maybe hide-and-seek wasn't such a bad idea. "This is a perfect house for it," she admitted. "There are a million great places to hide, all sorts of weird rooms to disappear in."

Alison shook her head. "It's *too* weird. Some pretty strange things have already happened. This house is spooky."

"I'm scared," Amber said in a small voice. "I don't think we should be running around here playing games. What if the people who live here catch us?"

"You're such a bunch of wimps," Matt declared. "I've never seen such cowards in my life."

"Cut it out, Matt," Chris said sharply. "Everyone's on edge."

"Well maybe you shouldn't be," Matt said. "Did you ever think of that? Maybe this is just an old house, and there's nothing to be scared of. Unless you're total wusses." His green eyes locked on Amber. "I dare you," he said softly. "I double dare you."

Amber shifted uncomfortably, her face red with shame.

"You, too, Alison," he said. "How come you and Amber always weasel out on dares? Maybe 'cause you're scared of your own shadows."

"That's not true," Heather said, coming to her friends' defense.

But Amber stood up angrily. "All right," she said. "I'll play your stupid game. At least I won't have to sit here in the same room with you!" She turned to Alison, her eyes pleading. "Come on, Ali. We *need* a distraction. Let's do it."

Matt grinned at Alison. "You're outnumbered, Comer." He stood up restlessly, and Heather knew a decision had just been made. None of them really got along with Matt, but he seemed to be the natural leader. "Anything's better than being bored crazy," he announced. "You four hide. I'll count to a hundred." He grinned again. "I'm going to enjoy getting all of you."

At his last words, Brian stirred and murmured as if at a sudden pain. Chris started over toward him, but Brian was already sleeping peacefully again.

"You better get a move on, Chris," Matt told him. Closing his eyes, he began counting.

Amber ran for the second floor. She knew where she wanted to hide. There was a big oak wardrobe in one of the bedrooms that she had been in earlier.

She headed down the left corridor, wondering how long it would it would take Matt to find her. Matt Field was the most obnoxious person she'd ever met. Once, right before a swim meet, he'd come up to her and said,

"Amber, can I talk to you for a minute? There's this question I've got to ask you." That was back when she didn't know Matt. Back then she actually thought he was cute. She'd felt flattered that he wanted to ask her a question. She remembered thinking that just maybe he thought she was cute, too. And she'd never forgotten his question: "So, Amber, are you *trying* to put on blubber like a seal?"

She knew why he gave her a hard time. Even though she was overweight, she always beat his times in the butterfly stroke. Matt Field couldn't stand a girl being better than him in anything.

Amber went all the way to the very last room in the corridor. She was sure Matt hadn't been in this one before. He'd been standing next to her when she first tried the doorknob. She hadn't been able to open it then. It had felt like it was locked. But later she'd tried the door again, and it had opened.

Now she tried the door for the third time. It opened easily. The room itself was very bare, almost grim. Amber's room at home was decorated with stuffed animals and bright posters. This room had a small white bed, a white ladder-back chair, and a plain wooden wardrobe. *I've seen more interesting potatoes,* Amber thought.

Feeling a little sorry for whoever had to sleep here, she went over to the wardrobe. Made of pale buffed pine wood, it was the nicest thing in the room.

Amber opened the tall door and leaned in to see if there was anything inside.

Suddenly something pushed her from behind. "Oww!"

she cried as she landed hard on her knees. She heard the door to the wardrobe slam shut at her back.

Amber forced herself to take a deep breath. "Don't panic," she told herself. She rubbed her sore knees. "Whatever you do, don't panic."

She twisted herself around and pushed against the door. It didn't move at all. Feeling across its back, she realized there wasn't a handle on the inside. It made sense, she supposed. After all, how many people got themselves trapped inside a wardrobe and had to open it from the inside? She pushed at the door again, and finally began pounding on it with both hands.

"Matt!" she yelled, hammering furiously. "I'm going to get you for this. Let me out of here, Matt! Open this door, you geek! Now!"

There was no sound in the room outside. But Matt *had* to be there. This was exactly the kind of disgusting trick he would play. None of the others would have even thought of it. "Matt!" she shouted again. "Let me out!"

Then she heard a sound. A soft, rhythmic pulsing. It was faint at first, right on the very edge of her hearing. It was the sort of sound you hear from your own heartbeat, only it wasn't hers. For a moment, she couldn't understand how she could hear anyone's heart if he were outside the closet. Then she realized the sound wasn't coming from the outside.

It was *inside* the wardrobe. With her.

Calm down, Amber, she told herself. *This wardrobe isn't big enough for more than one person.* But the rhythm went on, loud and clear and steady.

"Wh-who's there?" she asked in a thin, shaky voice.

With a bolt of courage she lunged across the darkness, trying to grab whoever was in there with her. Her hands hit wood on the side of the closet.

She was alone—except for the beat, which was growing louder each second.

Now she could hear her own heart, too, speeding up with fear. The thudding of the other heart was growing louder, pounding through the dark wardrobe. She could feel the wooden walls shaking with it. She was caught inside some huge, alien heart that was beating around her, trapping her.

She screamed again and pounded on the door, aware of another being. Not human at all, it was reaching out from some other place to capture her . . .

Suddenly the wardrobe door flew open. Amber tumbled out, shaken but relieved. The beating noise was gone, along with the feeling of an alien being.

"Gotcha!" Matt said, grinning down at her.

"Of course you did!" Amber shrieked. "You're the one who pushed me in there!"

"What are you talking about?" he asked, sounding surprised.

"You locked me in there!" Amber was yelling hysterically. "You sicko!"

He put up both hands, as if surrendering. "Whoa, Tubs. I only just got here. I was across the hallway when I heard you thumping and screaming. I thought it was a pretty weird way to play hide-and-seek, so I came to see what the problem was."

"*Somebody* locked me in the wardrobe," Amber insisted.

"So it has to be me?" Matt gave her an angry look. "I'm not responsible for *everything* bad, you know."

Amber felt her anger slipping away. Matt might be a jerk, but he didn't lie. Besides, he couldn't have made that weird pounding noise if he'd tried.

"There was something in the wardrobe with me," she said, trying to sound rational. "I could hear a heartbeat, and it was like . . . it surrounded me."

Matt raised an eyebrow and looked inside the wardrobe. "There's nothing there," he told her.

"There was."

"I doubt it." Matt grinned at her in his annoying way. "You must have heard your own heart in the darkness and gotten scared."

"That's not what it was," she said stubbornly.

Matt rolled his eyes. "All right," he said. "Maybe you did hear something, but there's no whatever-it-was, *no heartbeat* now."

Amber knew he was right. The sound was gone.

"Look," he said. "Why don't you come with me? I still have to find Heather, Alison, and Chris. Just don't lock yourself in any more wardrobes."

Amber's face went crimson. Matt had made her feel like a fool again. And she *hadn't* just heard her own heartbeat. She knew she hadn't. It was something else. But what?

Alison stood at the top of the stairs, wondering where she was going to hide. Once she'd decided to go ahead and play the game, or rather, once she'd let herself be guilted and shamed into playing, Alison refused to think about her fears. Anyway, Matt was probably right. She was just imagining things. After all, it was completely impossible: Brick walls don't just appear and disappear. Maybe she was suffering from post-stress syndrome or something, the result of the crash.

Still, the wall had *seemed* real. She shivered remembering it. She couldn't afford to think about it now, and she resolutely shoved the thought from her mind.

She looked around. What room would be her best—her safest bet—to hide in?

Amber was up here somewhere; she was pretty sure Heather and Chris were downstairs.

She could think of a few good places on this floor. She opened the door to the bedroom with the four-poster bed. She could slip inside the wardrobe and hide behind the clothes. But wardrobes were obvious places to look. Maybe she should try the bathroom, behind the screen. No, the screen didn't reach all the way to the floor. Matt would spot her there in a minute.

She tried the third door. It opened into the empty walk-in closet. There was nothing in the closet to hide her. As soon as Matt opened the door, he'd see her there. Then again, if she stood close to the door, Matt wouldn't be able to see her unless he actually stepped inside. And Matt always had been impatient. He'd probably peek in, see nothing, then go on.

Closing the door behind her, Alison pressed herself flat against the corner of the closet. Now all she had to do was to wait. . . .

There wasn't much light in the small space. Just a crack from under the door. How long would she be here? Just standing alone in the darkness. The idea was kind of scary. . . . *Stop that*, she told herself. There was nothing to be scared of. It was just an old closet. Except for her, it was empty.

And then Alison heard it. At first it was a faint vibration. She could feel it coming through the wall behind her. It was pulsing, a rhythmic trembling of the timbers of the house.

At the edge of her hearing, she could just make out noises. Footsteps as Matt searched farther down the hall. Amber's voice. He must have found her first.

But with those sounds there came another. One that at first she couldn't place. It was a pounding sound, faint at first, but growing louder with each passing second. *Thump . . . thump . . . thump . . .*

It was a heartbeat!

Calm down! she told herself sternly. *You're just hearing your own heart.*

Then why did the vibrations in the wall match the sound perfectly? Surely she wouldn't be feeling her own heart through the wall like that. She put one hand to her chest, trying to fight down rising panic. She could feel her own heart, pounding like mad.

And with a completely different rhythm from the one in the walls.

She jerked away from the wall, frightened. She couldn't feel the vibrations anymore, but the pounding still filled the air, getting louder.

She had to get out of this closet! She grabbed at the

door handle, trying to wrench it open to get back into the corridor.

The door didn't move. The handle turned, but the door remained shut tight. Desperately, she tugged harder, to no avail. She was trapped!

Alison let go of the handle and started hammering on the door. One of her friends would hear her and let her out. Matt would make fun of her, but even that would be better than being trapped in here. She had to get out—she had to!

''Matt!'' she screamed. ''Amber! Let me out of here!''

No one answered.

Alison heard herself screaming. It sounded odd. She knew she was making the sounds, but they seemed to be coming from a long way off. The room started to spin about her, and she screamed even louder.

Then there was a bright explosion of color that flooded her eyes, and she pitched forward into nothingness.

. . . SEEK . . .

Chris paused as he was about to enter the bedroom he'd chosen to hide in. Just for a second there he thought he'd heard a banging noise. Like someone knocking on a door. He waited for a few seconds, but the hallway was silent. He shrugged. He must've imagined it.

He reached for the doorknob again when he heard a faint scream that seemed to fade into nothing.

He stared down the corridor in the direction that the sound had come from. That was where Alison had gone to hide. At least, he was pretty sure it was Alison who'd raced up the stairs ahead of him and into the third door. Had she hurt herself? Why hadn't she cried out again? And why had it sounded so far away?

He was definitely imagining things. This house—this whole night—was giving him the creeps. Brian and his crazy ideas about Matt didn't help. Or Alison thinking she saw disappearing brick walls. Or the fire and candles lit by some mysterious, invisible host.

Then there was the thing *he'd* been feeling. He hadn't admitted it to the others. He didn't want to admit it to himself. But ever since they'd entered the house he'd had the feeling that they were being watched. The back of his neck had a funny feeling, as if eyes followed him wherever he moved. He spun around quickly. There was no one there, of course. Maybe he'd just seen too many horror movies.

He stepped into the bedroom. There it was again—that faint scream. The sound was so weak he couldn't be sure he really heard it. Imaginary or not, he knew he had to check it out.

He left the room and walked slowly down the corridor, stopping at the third door. He was pretty sure this was where he'd seen Alison go in.

He opened the door and peered in. "Alison?" he called softly. "You okay?"

There was no reply. He stared into what was obviously an empty closet.

"Alison," he called again, a bit louder. "It's Chris. Are you all right?"

There was still no reply. There was no sign at all of her having been in the small closet. He took a step inside and stared around. It was totally empty; even the shelves were bare.

Something tapped his shoulder.

Chris jumped, yelling, and spun around.

Matt grinned back at him. "Boy, you're touchy," he said. "And you didn't hide too well, either. You're out."

Chris took a deep breath, and felt his heart slowing back down to its normal rate. "I didn't know you were there," he said. His voice was shaking.

"Obviously," Matt agreed. "Or you'd have closed the

door at least. Let's look for the others now. I already found Amber.''

Chris was still uncertain. "What about Alison?"

"We'll get her next."

Chris stared around at the blank walls of the closet. "But I'm almost sure I saw her come in here. And I didn't see her leave."

Matt spread his hands. "Well, she *must* have left. She's not here now. If you seek as well as you hide, a herd of hippos could get past you."

"She never left this closet," Chris insisted.

"Right," Matt said. "She just turned invisible instead. Come on, dork, let's finish the game."

Amber peered inside the closet. "Ali? Are you there?"

Matt sighed wearily. "No. She's hiding someplace else. Now come on, you two dweebs, and we'll find her."

Maybe he *had* made a mistake, Chris thought. Maybe Alison slipped out when he wasn't looking. "Okay," he agreed. "Let's go." But he couldn't shake the feeling that they were making a major mistake.

Matt led the search. They looked in every room and wardrobe on the second floor, but there was no sign of Alison.

Matt simply shrugged. "Maybe she slipped downstairs while we were talking in the closet," he suggested. "Might as well look down there."

Feeling more and more uneasy, Chris and Amber followed Matt downstairs. They quickly found Heather in the kitchen, hiding in the pantry. Then the four of them searched the first floor. But no matter how hard or where they looked, they couldn't find Alison.

"Matt." Amber's voice was trembling. "This is getting scary. We should have found her by now."

"All right, all right. I know when I'm beat." Matt pushed a shock of dark hair out of his eyes. "Okay, Alison!" he yelled. "You win! I give up! Come on out!"

His voice echoed through the house.

Heather and Amber exchanged puzzled looks. Chris gnawed at his lower lip. "Something's seriously wrong," he said. "I'm pretty sure she went into that closet," he said. "And I'm pretty sure she didn't come out, either."

"Maybe there's some sort of secret panel in there," Amber suggested. "Don't old houses usually have that kind of thing? Maybe Alison found it and figured it was a neat place to hide. Or maybe . . . maybe she got stuck or something."

"Let's check it out," Chris said. He led everyone back upstairs and flung open the closet door. Nothing had changed. The small room was still bleak and empty.

Matt knocked against the walls. "I don't think there's room between the walls for a passage," he said. "This is a really stupid idea."

Chris felt his own temper rising. "Just look for something," he ordered.

Scowling, Matt started to rub the walls for cracks or hidden switches. "It's probably just some dumb joke she's playing on us," he muttered. "I'll bet she's waiting somewhere, laughing at us all right now."

"No, Matt," said Heather. "That's the way *you* act. Alison would never do that."

"Besides," Chris pointed out, "why hasn't she shown up to say she's won? If this *is* a joke, it's gone on too long."

They continued the hunt in silence. Amber and Heather even thumped the walls to try and see if they were hollow at any point. They weren't.

They finished going over the second floor for the third time. Amber sat down on the top of the staircase. She stared straight ahead and spoke in a wobbly voice. "When I was hiding I felt something in this house. It made a thumping sound like a giant heartbeat. Something besides us is in this house tonight. And I don't think it's human."

"Amber," Heather said softly. "What are you talking about?"

"I don't know," Amber said. "But I think it's got Alison."

"I think it's got your brain," Matt said.

"Give it a rest, Matt," Chris snapped. "This is not your normal suburban house, in case you haven't noticed. So far, we've all seen or felt some unusual things. It's not going to help if all we do is give each other a hard time about it." He turned to Amber. "Tell us what happened."

Amber tried to keep her voice calm. Still, she couldn't help quavering a little as she described how she'd been trapped in the wardrobe with the heartbeat, how the overpowering pulsing nearly drove her mad.

"It sounds bizarre," Heather said when she finished. "But I believe you."

"So do I," Chris said. "I just can't make any sense of it. I mean, could it really be a heartbeat? What could make a sound like that and be here in the house with us? And what does it have to do with Alison disappearing?"

"I think we'd all better be really careful," Heather said. "We shouldn't leave Brian alone for so long."

"Okay," Matt said quietly. "Let's go back down by the fire. If Alison *is* still hiding, she'll get tired of it soon. That's where she'll head, too."

Chris was the first one into the study. Brian was still in the chair by the fire. He was awake now, and he'd shifted his position a little. Chris took one look at his face and knew he was hurting bad.

"Did you try to stand up or something?" Chris asked.

"Just for a minute," Brian answered with a tight smile. "It didn't work too well." He tried to act nonchalant. "What's going on? I heard a lot of shouting. Or did I dream it?"

"Alison's missing," Heather told him. She sounded more than a little scared herself. "We were playing hide-and-seek, and now we can't find her."

Brian gave Matt a funny look, then huddled down further in the chair.

Matt didn't seem to notice the odd expression. "I'm going to check the road," he announced. "Just in case Mr. Clarke's back at the van looking for us." Heather and Amber wandered off after him and hovered in the doorway talking with each other.

"He'll see the lights from this house if he gets back," Chris pointed out. "When he doesn't see us at the wreck, he's bound to come up here after us."

"I need some air anyway," Matt said. Before anyone could protest he was on his way out.

Brian moved a little, and grimaced in pain. Chris crossed the room and knelt beside him. "Your leg looks swollen. It's worse, isn't it?"

"About the same. . . . You really can't find Alison?"

"No sign of her," admitted Chris. "It's pretty scary."

Brian looked nervous, then whispered: "I think Matt did something to her."

"What?" Chris stared at him in astonishment. "Matt?"

"*Shhh!*" Brian said in a panicky low voice. "Don't let him hear you!"

Chris dropped his voice. "What are you talking about?" he demanded.

"Well, when you were all in here earlier," Brian explained, "I was sort of half awake. It was his idea to play hide-and-seek, wasn't it? And I heard him mutter something about how he was going to get all of you."

Chris almost laughed. "He meant in the game, Brian. That he would find all of us in hide-and-seek."

"I don't think so," Brian replied, seriously. "He's never liked Alison, you know. Maybe he's already done something . . . something bad to her."

Chris shut his eyes. He didn't really want to hear this.

"Chris, I'm not making this up," Brian insisted.

"I know you're not," Chris said. "I'm just not sure what's real around here anymore."

"I'll show you what's real. Remember I told you I stood up for a minute? I saw something—proof that what happened before wasn't a dream. Go ahead. Look on top of the fireplace mantel and tell me what you see."

"Only to shut you up," Chris muttered. He stood up and felt his own eyes widen with fear. There on top of the mantel was a half-smoked cigar resting in a round metal ashtray.

Chapter Eight

SOUND, BUT NO SIGN

Chris felt as if he were reeling. The cigar and ashtray were real. Brian hadn't dreamed them. Did that mean that the dancing chair and Matt ripping off his face were real as well? They couldn't be, Chris told himself. Maybe the cigar and ashtray were sitting on the mantel all along. Maybe that's why Brian had a dream about them.

But someone had smoked the cigar, and not too long ago, by the looks of it. Where was that person? *Who* was that person? Chris shook his head to try to clear his thoughts. Right now he was sure of only one thing: something peculiar was going on.

"I'm telling you," Brian hissed urgently. "Matt caused the accident, and now he's done something to Alison."

"No," Chris insisted. "You know Matt didn't deliberately cause the accident. He couldn't have. And I don't think he'd deliberately hurt Alison."

"What are you two whispering about?" Heather asked, turning back into the room with Amber.

"Nothing," Chris said quickly.

"Alison," Brian said more honestly. "She couldn't have just vanished."

Amber sat down in the chair across from Brian. "I kind of thought there might be a secret passage from the closet, but there's no room on either side."

"Then maybe there's a trap door in the floor leading downstairs," Brian suggested.

That hadn't occurred to Chris. He'd assumed that a hidden exit or entrance would be in the walls. "That's an idea," he agreed. "What's underneath the closet?" He tried to visualize the plan of the house.

"I don't want to go up there again," Amber said quietly.

"I'll check it out," Chris said. He thought about the possibility of Matt coming back and upsetting Brian. "Will you two stay here with Brian?"

Heather nodded and Chris left the study. Just as he reached the main hallway, Matt came through the front door.

"Any luck?" Chris asked.

"I didn't see anything," Matt told him glumly. "No Coach and no other cars. We might as well be on the dark side of the moon for all the traffic around here."

Chris nodded. "I wonder what's taking Mr. Clarke so long. He should have been back here by now."

Shrugging, Matt replied, "Maybe they fixed the bridge and the cop left. Coach might have had to walk farther to find help." He stared at Chris. "You okay? You look kind of pale."

"I'm worried about Alison," Chris said. That was at least partly true. He didn't add: *And I'm trying to convince myself that you didn't have anything to do with it.*

"Yeah. It's pretty spooky." Matt ran his hand through his thick, dark hair. Then abruptly he said, "I don't like this house. There's too much going on that doesn't make sense."

Chris was amazed. Matt actually looked scared. And this was the first time he'd ever heard Matt admit he was worried about anything. "Mr. Clarke will be here soon with help," Chris said reassuringly. "We'll be fine."

"That's assuming we find Alison," Matt pointed out. "We can't just go off and leave her here, can we?"

"No," Chris answered. "Look, I'm going to check out the room under the closet. Brian thought there might be a trapdoor or something."

Matt shrugged again. "It's possible, I guess. I'll come with you. Between the two of us we'll get the search done faster."

Chris didn't know whether to be grateful for the offer—or terrified by it. He didn't really want to explore the old house by himself. But he didn't exactly trust Matt. One minute Matt was making everyone miserable. The next he was almost . . . nice. Then again, if he believed Brian, Matt was serious trouble.

"Uh—okay, thanks," Chris said, deciding he'd just have to be extra careful.

Together the two boys headed back across the main hallway and entered the other wing on the far side of the entrance hall. They walked to about where they thought the doorway to the closet would be on the floor above them. There was a large oak door in the wall before them.

"Weird," said Matt. "I don't remember this door being here when I was looking for Heather."

"Are you sure you came down this corridor?"

"Positive. And this door wasn't here."

Chris ignored the shivers that were running through him. "Well, let's see what's here now." He turned the knob and the door swung open.

"No way," Matt insisted. "This couldn't have been here before. One of us would have found it. We went through the whole house, remember?"

They were staring at a huge, formal dining room. In the center of the room was a long, polished wooden table. Fancy silver candelabras at either end of the table lit the room. Between the candelabras were six place settings, three on each side of the table. All of the plates were filled with food.

Matt slowly walked down the length of the huge table, his eyes fixed on the plates. Reluctantly, Chris followed him. Stopping by the first plate, Matt gingerly reached out and touched the edge of it.

"Cold," he said, sounding almost relieved.

"What did you expect?" Chris asked. "We've been here at least an hour, and we haven't seen anyone. Of course the food's cold. The people who live here must have left hours ago."

"Right in the middle of their dinner," Matt added. He pointed to the roast beef on the plate in front of them, which had been cut and partially eaten. The potatoes sat in congealed gravy.

"There were six of them, and there's six of us," Chris said quietly.

"So what?"

"I don't know," Chris admitted. "It just seems like a strange coincidence. Almost like we're taking their places or something. They're all gone. We're here, but now Alison's gone. Who's going to be next?"

"Aren't we supposed to be looking for a trapdoor?" Matt said gruffly. His eyes scanned the ceiling. "It looks pretty solid to me."

"Yeah," Chris agreed, craning his own neck to get a better look. "Let's just check around and make certain Alison hasn't been in here, though."

"If she had been, wouldn't she have come back to the study?" objected Matt.

"If she could," Chris agreed. "But what if she's in some hidden tunnel behind the walls or something? Maybe she can't get out."

"I think you've got a great imagination," Matt muttered, but he went to the wall and started banging. "Yo, Alison! You in there?"

As if to answer, a scream cut through the room, long and piercing.

Chris felt himself shaking. "That was Alison."

Matt looked up. "And she's somewhere right over our heads."

Chapter Nine

INSIDE AND OUT

For a long moment the echo of Alison's scream rang through the dining room. Chris looked at Matt and saw the same fear in Matt's eyes that he knew was in his own. "Alison's okay—or alive at least," Chris said. "She's still here somewhere. But she's in trouble."

Matt nodded. "So what are we waiting for?"

Together they turned and raced from the dining room, heading for the stairs.

They weren't the only ones who'd heard the scream. They met Heather and Amber running toward the stairs from the other wing of the house. Both girls looked pale and terrified.

"Is Brian okay?" Chris asked them.

Heather nodded. "He's asleep again. But we heard that scream—"

"The closet!" Chris said, and the four of them tore up the stairs.

Matt was the first to reach the closet. Behind him

Chris, Amber, and Heather stumbled to a halt as he threw open the door.

"I don't believe this," Heather said.

The closet was empty. There was no sign of Alison.

Chris took a deep breath to steady his nerves. He felt like screaming himself right about now.

"Where is she?" Amber asked in a whisper. "Did we all imagine that scream?"

"She's got to be here somewhere," Matt said. "We all heard her." He stepped into the closet, the others behind him. Matt and started pounding on the walls. "Alison, where are you?"

The only answer was the hollow echo of his own blows.

Matt turned to face the others. "She was here!" he insisted. "We all heard her!"

"Then where is she now?" Amber asked, near tears. She was shivering, Chris saw. Just like he was. And he knew it wasn't from cold. It was fear.

"If she's playing some kind of game—" Matt said angrily.

"She's not," Heather told him. "That was a real terror-in-your-guts scream."

"I know the feeling," Amber said miserably.

"Then keep it to yourself," Matt snapped as they stepped back out into the corridor. "We don't need you wimping out on us and making things worse."

"I'm not going to wimp out," Amber retorted. "I just want to know where my friend is."

"It's this house," Matt said.

"Don't start that again," Chris pleaded.

"Don't tell me what to do!" yelled Matt. He looked like

he was ready to punch Chris. "I *know* there's something wrong with this house. I can feel it. Alison's not the only one who's disappeared. What happened to the people who live here?"

"Maybe they went to a movie," suggested Amber hopefully.

"In the middle of dinner?" Matt scoffed. "We found the dinner table set and the food half eaten downstairs."

Amber's blue eyes widened with fear. "You mean . . . they vanished too?"

"It looks like it," Chris replied.

"Maybe they had the right idea," Matt said. "Maybe we ought to just get out of here while we still can."

"Not without Alison," Amber said. "We're not leaving her!"

"Of course not." Matt sounded disgusted. "We'll be heroic and stick around until we all vanish, one by one."

Chris felt the glimmer of an idea forming. "One by one," he repeated slowly. The others turned to look at him. "Maybe that's it," he said. "One by one."

"Talk English," Heather suggested.

Pointing to the closet door, Chris said: "Alison went into the closet on her own. I saw her. But none of us has gone in there alone since then. Matt was with me each time we checked it out, and the last time all four of us went in. Maybe whatever happened to Alison only works when one person is in the closet."

"That's really dumb," Matt said. "You think the closet cares how many people go into it? It's not alive, you jerk."

Amber stared at the door. "Maybe it's not so dumb,"

she said. "What if Chris is right? How do we get Alison out?"

"There's only one way I can think of," Chris said reluctantly. He didn't like the idea that had come to him at all. "One of us has to go in there—alone."

"No way," Matt said firmly. "I'm not even *thinking* of trying it."

"It was my idea," Chris said, wishing he felt braver. "I'll try it."

"You're crazy," Matt said. "You're just asking for trouble."

"Exactly," Chris agreed. "I'm asking for whatever happened to Alison."

Brian stood beneath the balcony and drew deep breaths of cold, wet air. The fever made him woozy. Chills raced up his spine. The pain in his leg was worse than anything he'd ever imagined. But he was out of the house. Forcing each step, he stumbled out into the storm.

He could barely see through the slashing rain. He had no idea of where he was going. All he knew was he had to get away from the house.

They'd left him alone in the study again. This time a book had flown down from the shelves and opened itself in his lap. Afraid of what he'd see, he'd tried not to look at it. He'd just pushed himself out of the chair and, step by painful step, had dragged himself out of the house.

Brian pushed a shock of soaking wet hair from his eyes. Where was the road anyway? It was right in front of the house. At least, that's what he remembered. He moved in as straight a line as he could. He'd find the road, and the others would find him there. Even if he drowned, it would be better than sitting in that study with everything flying through the air.

He hadn't gone that far when his shin hit something. Brian swayed for a moment and then lost his balance. He cried out as he landed hard on the muddy ground. For a few minutes, the pain in his leg was so bad, he couldn't see.

I'll never make it home again, Brian thought. He tried not to cry and then decided it didn't matter. No one would ever find him out here, and his face was wet from the rain anyway. For a long while he just sat there sobbing.

At last the tears stopped. Brian wiped his nose and looked around for something that would help him stand up. And then he saw what it was he'd stumbled on. Directly in front of him a worn rectangular piece of stone jutted up from the earth.

Brian pulled himself toward it. If he could hold onto it, he might be able to pull himself up. Sliding on his side, he reached out for the stone. His fingers closed around its edge.

He managed to get his good leg beneath him. Slowly, he started to stand. He froze as a flash of lightning showed him what lay on the other side of the stone. He was looking down into an open grave. The stone he was holding on to was a tombstone.

The scream that began in his throat died as lightning again streaked the sky. And Brian realized that there were *six* tombstones. Six graves. And in each one was an open, empty casket. Waiting.

INTO THE CLOSET

Chris stared at the closet door, feeling his heart pound. What had he just agreed to? Alison was trapped somewhere inside the house. And he was volunteering to be trapped along with her.

"Chris, don't." Heather put her hand on his arm. "What if you vanish too?"

"At least you'll know how I vanished," Chris replied. "And hopefully I'll find Alison. Wherever she is." He shrugged, trying to act a whole lot more casual than he felt. "Maybe if I find her, we can figure out some way to escape together."

"If she's not a ghost, too, by now," Matt broke in. "Maybe that's why we can't see her. Maybe she's dead and haunting this house."

Amber shuddered at the thought. "Don't even *say* that! It's just too horrible to think about."

Chris knew he couldn't put it off any longer. He took a candle from the candlestick in the hallway and stepped back inside the empty closet. Before closing the door, he turned back to his friends. "Keep talking while I'm in there," he said. "I'll answer you. That way I won't feel so out of touch."

Gathering every ounce of courage he still had, Chris took two steps into the closet and pulled the door shut behind him.

"Chris!" It was Amber's voice. "Is everything all right?"

"Yeah," he called back. "I'm fine." The flickering candle made the shadows jump, but it was just a closet. He felt a little silly. "Nothing's happening at all."

A sudden breeze snatched at his skin, raising goose-bumps. Chris frowned. Where could a gust of wind come from in here? His heart started to beat faster.

Matt's voice came through the door behind him. "See any ghosts yet?"

"I don't see anything, but . . ." Chris stopped speaking as another gust of wind whipped around him. The flame on the candle flickered and then died. Terrific, he thought. His eyes held the blurry afterimage of the flame, but he couldn't see a thing in the darkness.

"What happened?" Amber yelled through the door.

"The candle—" Chris began as he started to turn. Then he lost his footing somehow, and everything fell away from him.

Brian tried to scream, but only a high choking sound came out. His voice wouldn't work. And that scared him almost as badly as the six gaping graves.

Those graves are waiting for us, he thought wildly. *Someone dug those graves for us!*

He managed to push himself to a standing position.

He knew he had to warn the others. He could feel his chest tightening with fear. The last thing in the world he wanted to do was to go back into that house. He wasn't even sure he could make it that far. But he had no choice. Chris had been his best friend since the third grade.

Painfully, he began to make his way back to the house. It wasn't that far, but his leg throbbed horribly with each step. He was burning up with fever, shaking with cold. And the storm was howling. Brian could almost believe it was laughing, mocking him for being foolish enough to think he could survive this night.

He fell again just as he reached the front of the house. For a moment he lay in the rain, not moving, waiting for the pain to ease. He wiped his eyes with the back of his hand. He was sobbing again.

Get a grip, he told himself sternly. *You're only a few feet from the door. You can't let the others see you this way.*

Just a few feet away was one of the pillars that supported the balcony. He could use the pillar to pull himself to his feet. He inched over to the pillar, and at its base he saw a cement plaque, edged in brass. There were three lines of raised letters he could just make out:

Campbell House
Built September 5, 1825
Destroyed by fire April 25, 1864

He looked up at the massive house above him. Apparently, there had been another built here before this one. This one must have been put up sometime after 1864.

This is like a commercial, Brian thought hysterically. *I'm soaking wet, feverish, in pain, and scared out of my mind. And we take a break for a history lesson.*

He reached for the pillar to pull himself up—and this time his hands dug into the rough upholstery on the arm of the wing chair. Brian blinked and tried to sit up, grimacing as the pain hit.

It was another crazy fever dream, he realized. His heart was pounding, and he was alone in the study again. And though he was soaking wet, it was from sweat, not rain. He'd never left the chair. He'd never seen six open graves. He'd never read a historical plaque explaining there'd been another house here.

Then why did it all seem so real? He knew it was every bit as real as the floating cigar. He was sure that if he could walk outside he'd find the plaque. And the graves.

His terror came back full force as he pictured the six open graves. That's when he noticed something heavy in his lap. He looked down and nearly screamed. It was the book he'd dreamed of, the one that flew down from a shelf.

Now it lay open in his lap to an old-fashioned woodcut. The illustration showed a skeleton lying in an open coffin. Beneath the print, the old-fashioned printing read: *There is no one of us who escapes.*

_____

Amber grabbed the door knob and twisted hard. The closet door didn't budge. "Chris," she shouted. "What's happened?"

Chris didn't answer.

Amber struggled with the door again. "It's stuck."

"Let me try," Matt said. With a hard yank he jerked open the door.

Amber, Heather, and Matt stared. Then Amber gasped and began to sob. The closet was empty. Chris was gone.

Chapter Eleven

ALISON!

Lightning flashed in the distance, breaking the thick gloom of . . . of *wherever* he was. Chris's first thought as he slipped and slid down the bumpy slope was that there *was* a secret tunnel to the outside. He was being dumped out into the storm.

Then, still skidding over rocks and stones, he realized how impossible that was. The light of the flash died away, allowing the blackness to return. This wasn't the same storm. A low rumble of thunder shattered his thoughts for a second. But there was no rain. Just wind and lightning and thunder.

The ground he was sliding over was bone dry. Wherever he was, no rain had fallen in this place in a long time.

With a bone-jarring thump, he slammed to a stop against a large rock. The impact sent a flare of pain through his chest and left arm. Wincing with pain, he gathered his feet under him and managed to stand up, swaying.

He felt nauseated and a little giddy. The air smelled funny—stale and musty, the sort of smell that old

69

books have. Even the lightning was odd. It gave off a strange silver-purple light. Seconds after the flare itself had died away, everything around him still held the silver-purple glow.

He took a few deep breaths until he stopped being afraid he'd fall over if he moved. He waited for his eyes to adjust to the darkness. The only sound he could hear was the crash of thunder that accompanied each stab of lightning.

He peered back the way he had come, half expecting to see the boards of the floor somewhere behind and above him. But he could see very little in this darkness. He wondered if it was dark because of the strange storm or because it was night.

Or because this place didn't have a sun.

That's impossible, he told himself. I must be getting light-headed. Maybe it was this tired air he was breathing. He started walking back toward the house. Or what should be back toward the house.

What did he think had happened anyway? That he'd fallen through some sort of hole in space that just happened to be located in the floor of a closet? He remembered seeing something like that once on an old episode of *The Twilight Zone*. But that was a TV show. *This* was for real.

His eyes had adjusted a little to the darkness and lightning now. The ground itself was light and sandy. Huge boulders littered the weird landscape. Some were shaped like giant tortoises, others like sleeping bears. In the flickering light they almost looked alive.

"Well, Toto," Chris muttered to himself, "I have a

feeling we're not in Kansas anymore.'' He'd spoken just to hear a voice, even if it was his own.

When he and Brian were ten, they'd taken a dare to spend an hour in a cemetery at midnight. That's what this place felt like, he realized with a chill. He remembered how he and Brian had been sure they heard ghosts calling in the wind. They'd even whistled all of ''The Star Spangled Banner'' to keep from panicking. They'd told each other over and over that there was no such thing as ghosts, but neither one of them had ever been so scared in his life. Until tonight.

He jumped as he heard a scratching sound about twenty feet away. The hairs on the back of his neck literally started to rise, and he felt a shiver of pure terror shake him. He was no longer sure that ghosts didn't exist.

''Chris?'' asked a quivering voice. ''Chris? Is that you?''

Relief flooded through him. ''Alison!'' he yelled. ''Alison! I'm over here.'' He'd found her! He was right. She *had* come through the closet to . . . well, here.

''Keep your voice down!'' she hissed. He could hear her scrambling across the rocks toward him. Then he made out her shape in the gloom. He staggered across the strange ground to meet her halfway.

Almost before he knew it, Alison grabbed hold of him. She clung to him, almost crushing the breath out of him.

''Hey, it's okay,'' he said gently. He knew why she was acting like this. He'd been here just a few minutes, and this place was freaking him out. Alison must've been here all alone for almost an hour. She must have been going nearly crazy by now.

"Can I breathe now?" he teased her after a minute.

"Oh." Embarrassed, Alison relaxed her grip. But she held onto his arm, as if she were afraid he'd vanish if she let go. And as far as Chris knew, he might. The rules he'd always taken for granted were no longer working. Anything could happen. The word *normal* no longer applied.

"Where are we?" he asked.

"I don't know," she whispered. He could just about make out the terrified expression on her face. "It's something out of a nightmare. One second I was in the closet back in the old house. . . . Then I was *here.*"

"Yeah," he said, slowly. "That's what happened to me. I closed the closet door, and then I was falling. I landed here. Is this where you were when you were screaming?"

Alison nodded.

"Then we've got to still be somewhere near the house. We could hear you in there, even though you sounded kind of muffled."

The thunder crashed again, louder than before. Chris jumped, but Alison didn't even seem to notice. "You get used to it," she explained. "After you've been here a few hours, the thunder isn't so scary."

Chris almost missed what she had said. Then he blinked. " 'A few hours'? Alison, you've only been gone about forty minutes or so, tops."

"What?"

"How long do you think you've been here?" Chris asked warily.

"About ten hours," she replied. She held up her arm

72

and pointed to her digital watch. "It's eight in the morning. I know, because I've spent a lot of those hours watching the minutes tick by."

Chris held up his own watch and read it by the next flash of lightning. "It's almost ten o'clock at night."

"Your watch must be broken," she insisted.

"I don't think so. Let's face it. Everything else in this place is so screwy, it figures that even time isn't the same."

"I don't know if we can get back," Alison said softly.

"Of course, we can," Chris told her. "We just go back up the hill behind us. We're bound to find the closet again sooner or later."

"What hill?" Alison asked.

"This—" He turned to gesture behind him at the slope he'd skidded down when he fell through the closet floor. His mouth fell open. The ground behind him was as flat as that in front of him. There wasn't any slope.

"I've looked for a way," Alison said. "And everywhere I look there's empty ground and boulders. I've been hunting for that closet for at least ten hours. I must have walked miles. It's endless."

"It can't be," Chris said.

Alison didn't answer, and he knew she was right. They weren't in the house. And they weren't exactly out of it. They were caught in some other place, farther from their own world than they'd ever been. And there was no route back.

Another forked tongue of lightning lit up the place and then died.

"I don't get it," Chris said. "Somehow, whatever this place is, it's connected to the house." He felt a shudder go through him. "I wonder if the people who lived in the house disappeared the same way we did."

Alison's voice became even quieter. "It does feel like somebody planned it."

"Somebody?" he echoed. "Is there someone else here, too?"

Her hand tightened its grip on his arm. "I don't know if it's a some*body* or some*thing*. But every now and then I can feel it moving. Actually, *them* moving. I think there's more than one."

Chris peered into the darkness. Of course, he saw only more rocks. "One what?" he asked.

"I don't know exactly."

"Well, then where are they? Whatever they are."

"Out there. Sometimes I can hear them." She said it so casually that for a second he wondered if Alison wasn't losing it. "That's why you have to keep your voice down. If we can hear them, they can probably hear us."

Chris felt his heart racing again. He held his breath, listening. All he could hear was his own frantic heartbeat.

Suddenly Alison nodded. In the silence, he strained to listen.

She was right. From somewhere off in the gloom, he could hear the sound of something rustling across the ground, then the sound of pebbles bouncing as they were dislodged.

Something was stalking them in the darkness.

Chapter Twelve

MATT'S MOVE

Matt sank down against the wall in the upstairs corridor and shut his eyes. He hadn't really expected Chris to disappear. But he should have. Enough weird stuff had gone on tonight for him to expect just about anything. Rooms appeared and disappeared. Why shouldn't people?

"Matt." Heather was standing over him, her hands on her hips. "Are you going to just sit there?"

"I don't know," he said quietly. For once he had no plans.

Amber looked at the closet and shuddered. "Chris was right. There's definitely something odd about this closet. . . . Maybe we should search it again for a hidden door." She didn't look at all eager to try it.

"There isn't much point," Matt replied. "We've already looked twice and found nothing."

"Then what are we going to do?" Heather's voice was

shrill and dangerously near to cracking. "We can't just leave them!"

Matt gave her a strained look. "Why not?" he asked. "They've vanished, and we don't know where or how. The smartest thing to do would be to go for help."

Amber glared at him. "How can you even *think* of leaving them?" she demanded. "They're our friends!"

"They're *your* friends," Matt pointed out grimly. "If you want to go in after them, I won't stop you." He gave her a thin smile. "Of course, I doubt you'll come out again."

Amber looked terrified, and Heather looked as if she wanted to strangle him. Neither girl looked as if she was willing to do as he suggested.

"Look," he said after a short pause, "I'm worried about them, too. But I'm serious—probably the best thing that we can do is to get help. This whole situation is out of hand. It's gone way beyond spooky."

"That's why we can't go for help," Heather replied firmly. "Alison and Chris could be in major trouble right this second. We can't afford to waste time looking for help. You know it could take forever. Coach *still* hasn't come back, and he's been gone for *hours!*"

"Alison and Chris probably *are* in trouble," Matt agreed. "And if we go in there one at a time, we'll just add to the number of idiots in danger." He glanced into the empty closet again and shook his head. "I'm not dumb enough to do that."

"Of course not," Amber snapped. "You're too self-ish."

Matt gave a snort. "I'm being practical. We need some kind of plan to give us a fighting chance. There's no sense in one more person getting lost. If you come up with a plan, let me know. Until then I'm not going in there."

"So who needs you?" asked Heather, turning her back on him. "Amber and I can figure something out, right?"

"Right." But Amber didn't sound very sure of herself. Matt couldn't resist a snicker.

Heather just tossed her head, flicking her long, dark hair in disgust. "There has to be some sort of hidden trapdoor or something," she told Amber. "Maybe it only works when the door is closed."

Matt was pretending not to listen, but he had to admit that Heather had a point. He wasn't quite as unconcerned about Alison and Chris as he pretended. If he was honest with himself, he did kind of like them both. And they probably *were* in serious trouble right now.

"Suppose you're right," he said suddenly. "What if there is a trap, and it's set off by closing the closet door?"

Heather didn't turn round. "I thought you weren't interested in helping."

"I didn't say that," he objected. "I said I wasn't doing anything without a plan. And I think I've just had an idea. We'll need a length of rope," he went on. "If there is some sort of trap in the closet, it has to open sideways or downward. Maybe it's a fall of some kind."

Amber paled. "You think Ali and Chris may have fallen to their deaths?"

"No." Matt shook his head. "We know Alison survived the fall because she screamed later. I think it's just too far for them to be able to get back up on their own. Maybe it's a slide into the basement, or something.''

''Maybe,'' admitted Heather. She gave him a look of grudging respect. ''So we throw them a rope. How?''

''Well, not throw them one, exactly,'' Matt answered. ''I kind of figured that we'd have to take it to them. We tie one end to the doorknob, and the other around the waist of . . . one of us. Then we close the closet door.''

Amber looked at Heather, then back at Matt. ''So . . . which one of us volunteers to try it?''

Matt scuffed at the floor with the toe of his sneaker. ''It's my idea,'' he said reluctantly. ''So I guess it should be me.''

Brian sat staring into the fire. The book that had mysteriously appeared on his lap lay on the floor. He'd almost thrown it in the fire, then realized he couldn't. The book was proof that he wasn't imagining things and he wasn't going crazy. He needed it to convince the others that they had to get out of this house soon. Before it was too late.

Brian didn't have a watch, but he knew they'd been gone for a while now. He was pretty sure they hadn't found Alison. Someone would have told him if they had. What happened to her? he wondered. Was she still alive?

Since his last dream, he wasn't so sure Matt was to blame for Alison's disappearance. Brian still blamed Matt for the accident and his broken leg. But whatever was going on in this house was much bigger than Matt Field. Or the Matt Field he *thought* he knew.

The trouble was Brian couldn't sort out his dreams from reality. He thought he'd dreamed the floating cigar and the flying book. He had proof that both of them were real. So what did that tell him about Matt and the six open graves?

He ought to try to get outside and check. But his leg was throbbing, sending fiery waves of pain through him. It scared him to be sitting here with a broken leg, not knowing when or *if* he'd get help. Even scarier was the feeling of helplessness. The six of them were trapped here, Brian was sure of it. Someone or some-*thing* was keeping them prisoner. And there was nothing he could do.

Once again Brian's eyes came to rest on the ornate fireplace mantel. And again he had the feeling that the carved figures were really dancing. They seemed to be mocking him. They were wood, but they could move; he was human and he was stuck.

Stop it! Brian told himself sternly. You don't need another fever dream. But the figures continued to dance. Men bowed to women. Women curtsied and whirled. If he listened hard enough, he thought he could hear music playing in the distance.

Then he heard a creaking sound that he knew was real. On the right side of the room one of the heavy bookcases suddenly slid away from the wall behind it. Behind it was a wooden panel. Brian watched in disbelief as the panel slowly slid back. *A secret passage!* he thought. He'd found a secret passage!

"The problem is," Matt explained to Heather and Amber, "I don't know where we're going to find a rope. I've been all through this house and haven't seen one."

"No problem," Amber said. "We could use that old trick—tie sheets together. There're loads of sheets up here."

"I should have thought of that," Matt muttered. Then he gave her a half grin. "Well, since that's *your* idea, you want to be the one to try the closet next?"

"No thanks," Amber said quickly. "I'll pass on that one."

"Let's get busy," Heather suggested. "If Ali and Chris are in trouble, the sooner we get to them the better."

They went into the nearest bedroom. The two girls stripped the bed while Matt rummaged through the chest at the foot of the bed. They managed to get half a dozen sheets and took them back to the open closet.

Matt pulled a penknife from his pocket, and they began to cut the sheets into thick strips and knot the pieces together. Finally, they had a "rope" that was about a hundred feet long.

"I guess this is long enough," Matt said. Part of him wished they could go on knotting the rope forever. He wasn't looking forward to what came next.

"Are you sure it's long enough?" Heather asked.

"I'm not sure of anything," Matt replied. "But I figure we don't have that many options. May as well try it." He tied one end of the sheet-rope around his chest, just under his arms. The other end he fastened to the inside door-knob on the closet.

He really didn't want to do this. None of them knew what might happen once the door was closed. But he had to try, and waiting wasn't making him any braver.

"Okay," he said. He gathered up the sheet-rope in his arms. "I'm going in. Amber, when I give you the word, close the door."

"And then?" she asked. She looked scared.

He shrugged. "We see what happens. From Chris's experience, I'd say if anything *does* happen, I won't be able to call out. Give me ten seconds with the door closed, then try and open it again."

He stepped into the closet. It took all his courage just to get his feet to move. He was terrified, but he wasn't about to let Heather and Amber know that. He stood in the center of the closet, the rope tightly gripped in both hands.

Taking a deep breath, he nodded at Amber. "Go ahead."

"Are you sure you're ready?" she asked.

"No. But I won't get more ready waiting around. Just do it."

Amber swallowed nervously, then nodded.

Matt watched as the door slammed shut, cutting off the outside world and all light. For a second, in the blackness, he felt like screaming.

Then he *did* scream as the floor dropped out from below him and he began falling into the darkness.

Chapter Thirteen

THE NIGHTMARE ZONE

"What is making those sounds?" Chris whispered.

"I don't know," Alison said softly. "And I'm not sure I want to." She let go of his arm and peered into the darkness. Thunder rumbled and another flash of lightning lit the scene for an instant. Then the thunder died down and they heard the sounds again. "It almost sounds like some kind of fabric making that rustling noise," Alison said. "And the pebbles scattering sound like—"

"Footsteps."

She nodded. With Chris here, she wasn't quite as terrified as she'd been alone. She glanced at him again. The light was poor, but she could see that his face was drawn. He looked as scared as she was.

For long moments both of them listened as the sounds seemed to fade into the distance. "They're still out there somewhere," Chris said in a whisper. "But it sounds like they're farther away. Do you have any idea what they are?"

"No." She bit her lip to stop it from trembling. Chris

was standing here, asking her rational questions, like this whole strange scene was some kind of regular mystery they could solve if only they had the right clues. She couldn't bear to tell him it wasn't like that here. She wished she could answer his questions and suddenly have all their problems solved. But it was hard to pretend things would be okay. She felt raw and exhausted, as if something inside her was close to breaking point.

"Have you seen anything alive in here?" Chris asked.

"Only you," she replied. "Look." She knelt down, overturned one of the smaller rocks, and waited for a flare of lightning to show him what she'd found. "See, it's just this gray dust. No bugs . . . or, or anything. No plants. No people. Except us," she finished miserably.

"Maybe not *right* here," Chris said.

Alison could tell he was trying to be reassuring. "Not anywhere here!" she insisted. "I've been walking and walking. This entire place is dead."

"Except for whatever is making those sounds," he added thoughtfully. "I don't know, Ali, but I think the only thing to do is try and find our way back to the house."

Alison silently counted to ten, telling herself not to scream. "What do you think I've been doing?" she finally asked.

"Sorry," he said quickly. "But this place has to connect up with the closet somehow. We both got here that way, right? We ought to be able to retrace our steps."

"Okay," she said patiently. "Which direction would *you* go in?"

Chris scanned the dark horizon for a moment before

answering. "Well, I'd . . . I'd look for our footprints. With all of this dust, we must have left footprints. All we have to do is to track them back."

Shaking her head, Alison patted him gently on the arm. "Believe it or not, that was one of the first ideas I had, too." She stared out at the rocky desert. There were no footprints, of course. "If we leave footprints in this place, and I'm not sure we do, the wind erases them. I tried making lines in the dirt. I even tore up a piece of paper that was in my pocket and tried leaving bits of it under rocks for a trail. It doesn't matter what you do—inside a few minutes, everything's back the way it was before."

"Maybe if we use the rocks themselves to make markers—" Chris began.

"I don't think it will work," Alison said. "But I'm willing to try."

They gathered together a small pile of stones. "Okay," Chris said. "Let's call this marker our starting point. We'll walk twelve paces and make another one."

Alison said nothing but walked the twelve paces with him and helped gather another pile of stones. Then they walked twelve more paces and built a third marker.

"All right, now," Alison said. "We haven't gone very far. Only twenty-four paces. Let's try to find those markers."

Chris turned around. In the glow of a lightning flare he gave a cry of disbelief. "They're gone!"

Alison decided it would be tacky to say "I told you so."

Chris kicked at a rock. "How could they just be gone?" he demanded. "The wind isn't that strong!"

"I don't think the normal physical rules apply here," Alison reminded him. "Remember, time is different. And so is everything else. Night without end. Storms without rain."

"Then we're stuck," Chris said bitterly. "There's no sun or trees to use as guides, and nothing stays where you put it. We could stumble around in this wilderness forever and just be walking in circles! We're stranded in this . . . this nightmare zone. There's no way we'll ever get out."

Alison felt her own temper rising. "That's just great! I really needed someone to come all the way down here to tell me things are even worse than I thought. Why'd you go into the closet anyway?"

Chris gave her a crooked grin. "Would you believe I thought I was rescuing you?"

For the first time in hours Alison laughed. She laughed until she was gasping for breath.

"All right already," Chris finally said. "It's not *that* hilarious. But you're right. Coach keeps telling us that the only losers are the ones who give up."

Alison stopped laughing. She really was losing it. Everything was absurd, and she was giving in. She had to get control. She took a deep breath. "Coach is right," she said. "And we've never been losers before."

"No," he agreed. "So let's pick a direction. Which way?"

"Left," she told him, still feeling giddy. "I'm left-handed, and I feel lucky."

She started off in the direction of a large boulder,

promising herself that she'd keep a grip on things. Chris fell into step beside her.

"Uh, Alison," he said after they'd been walking a while. "I'm not sure this is such a lucky direction."

She stopped walking at once and listened. The strange sounds were back again. In a flare of silver-purple light, she saw Chris's eyes go wide with terror.

"What is it?" she asked as the darkness returned.

He put a hand out to stop her. "Just don't go any farther," he whispered. "Maybe we ought to turn around."

"Why?" she demanded. "At least tell me what you saw."

The next flash of lightning gave her the answer.

A little ways ahead of them stood a circle of boulders. And lying in the center of the circle were six human skeletons.

Alison forgot all about self-control and screamed her head off.

Chapter Fourteen

THE SECRET PASSAGEWAY

Heather stared at the inside of the closet door. The rope was still tied to the knob, but Matt was gone. The rope itself seemed to go straight through the floorboards.

Beside her Amber had gone a sickening shade of gray. "What did we just do?" she asked.

"I don't know," Heather replied. "I never thought I'd be sorry to see Matt Field vanish, but—"

"It's not funny, Heather! First Alison, then Chris, now Matt!" Amber's voice was rising with hysteria. "We knew for pretty sure Alison disappeared here. Then we lost Chris. Then we let Matt go, too. Matt didn't want to. He knew it would be useless. And we let him go anyway! What if they never come back?"

Heather had never seen Amber so upset. Carefully, she shut the closet door. "First thing is, no one else is going in there," she said. She put an arm around her friend. "The second is, you and I have to figure something else out fast."

Amber was sobbing now. "We can't leave them."

"I'm not sure we can stay either," Heather told her. "I'm beginning to think Matt was right. We've got to get help. Staying in this house is only making things worse. *Seriously* worse."

Amber wiped her eyes on her sleeve. "What about Brian? We can't leave *him.*"

Heather thought carefully before answering. Everything in her wanted to race straight out the front door and keep going. She didn't care if she was running into the middle of a hurricane or even a blizzard. Something told her that they didn't have much time left in this house. If they didn't get out soon, they never would. The question was, if they took Brian with them, would they get out soon enough?

"Come on," Amber said firmly, her tears gone. "We're going downstairs to get Brian now." She turned to head back down the hall.

Heather put a hand on her friend's arm. "Listen to me. We can't fool around any longer. We've got to get out of here *fast.* Brian's in really bad shape. We may not be doing him any favors by asking him to move. We might be making things worse for him."

Amber looked at Heather as if she were seeing a monster. "You're afraid he'll slow us down, aren't you?" She took a step back from her friend. "What's gotten into you?" she asked. "I thought *Matt* was the selfish one."

Heather took a deep breath. "We can't afford—"

"We can't afford to leave him here!" Amber finished angrily. "Heather, if I was the one with the broken leg, would you run out on me?"

"Of course not!" Heather said.

"Then we can't leave Brian. Or *you* can if you want. I'm going to get him out of here."

Stunned, Heather watched as Amber raced down the corridor ahead of her. She and Amber had never had a fight before. Actually, before this insane night, she couldn't remember Amber arguing with *anyone*.

"Amber, wait!" she cried, running after her. She trailed her friend down the staircase, and through the corridors to the study.

Ahead of her, Amber skidded to an abrupt halt. She turned back toward Heather, a puzzled expression on her face. "The st-study," she began uncertainly.

"Oh, no," Heather said.

Amber pointed to the wood-paneled wall in front of them. "There was a doorway right here, wasn't there?"

Everything else was the same. The door to the study had been flanked by two small half-circle tables. One held a brass candlestick with lighted candles. The other held a blue-and-white china vase. The tables were still there. And so were the candlestick and the vase. But between them, where a doorway had stood, was solid wall.

"Brian!" Amber began to pound on the wall. "Are you in there?" She turned to Heather frantically. "Help me call him!"

The two girls called until they were hoarse.

If Brian was in the sealed study, he never answered. Or he couldn't hear them.

At last Amber wore herself out. She leaned against the wall, defeated. "Tell me I'm not going crazy," she said.

Heather couldn't find her voice. She had no idea who or what was crazy anymore.

"The door into the study is gone," Amber went on. "There used to be a doorway here, and now there isn't one. Brian was in there! Now we don't know where he is!" She looked at Heather, tears in her eyes. "We're never going to get out of this place, are we?"

Brian pinched himself hard to make sure he was awake. He grabbed onto the arms of the wing chair. He tugged on a strand of hair. He even made sure both eyes were open. As far as he could tell, he wasn't dreaming. And the secret passage behind the bookshelves was still open.

He craned his neck trying to peer inside. It didn't work. His chair was at the wrong angle.

Slowly, Brian pushed himself to a standing position. He didn't know who or what had opened the secret panel. He had a wild hope that maybe Alison was back there. Maybe she'd opened the panel from the other side.

He swayed a little. It was hard balancing on one foot, especially when the fever made him dizzy. He reached for the fireplace poker. Using it as a cane, he began to make his way across the room.

Finally Brian was standing in front of the open panel. He couldn't see the control anywhere on the bookshelves. And he couldn't see inside the passageway. It was completely dark. "Alison," he called out. "Alison, are you in there?"

He wasn't really surprised when Alison didn't answer.

Brian moved a little closer to the passage. His leg was

hurting like crazy, but his curiosity was even stronger. He took a candle from one of the shelves and held it in the opening of the passage.

He was looking into a tunnel of some sort. The walls seemed to be made of stone. Did it go under the house, he wondered. For the hundredth time that night, Brian wished he hadn't broken his leg. He was sick of hurting so badly. He was so sick of sitting in that chair by the fire, waiting for everyone else to tell him what was going on. He knew what was going to happen. Matt would come down to the study first. He'd see the open panel and then tell everyone how he had been the first to check out the secret passageway.

"So you found it," said a soft voice behind him. "And here I thought you were too stupid to find your nose."

Brian turned to see Matt standing there, his face unnaturally white.

"H-how'd you get in here?" Brian asked. "And how did you know about the passageway?"

"Never mind that, you dweeb. Do you want to see what's in there? Or are you too much of a wimp to leave your cozy fire?"

Brian would never trust Matt. "Why don't you just tell me what's in there?"

"No can do," Matt told him. "See for yourself or you'll never know."

"What happened to Alison?" Brian asked him.

Matt gave a lazy shrug. "Does it matter?"

Brian stepped back as Matt moved closer to him. There was something wrong with Matt's face, Brian realized.

The skin was stretched so tightly across the bones, it looked like a mask.

But the voice couldn't have belonged to anyone but Matt: "I'll tell you a secret, lame brain. This passageway is the only way out of this house. Alison didn't find it. And Chris won't. But I'm here to give you one last chance."

Brian stood paralyzed with fear. He didn't even know what he was looking at. Was it really Matt, and if it was, what had happened to him? And was he telling the truth?

Matt leaned against a bookshelf, his arms folded. "This is getting boring, Bri," he said. "Either you go into the tunnel there and we get out of this trap—or you stay. For good. Now which is it going to be?"

Brian didn't answer.

"Can't make a decision?" Matt asked. "Guess I'll have to make it for you. You're going into the tunnel."

He moved closer to Brian, backing Brian toward the tunnel. He was only inches from the threshold now. From within the dark passageway Brian heard something pulsing, like the rhythm of a heartbeat. It gave him a sick feeling that had nothing to do with his fever or his leg. "What's that noise?" he asked.

Matt's smile was mocking. "Haven't you guessed by now? It's the house."

"Houses don't have heartbeats," Brian argued.

"This one does. Haven't you figured it out yet, stupid? It's alive! And it's going to keep you and all your wimpy friends. You're never getting out."

"What about you?" Brian asked, his voice shaking.

"Not an issue," Matt told him. "It's already got me.

Watch." Again Matt reached his hand up, and once again he pulled the flesh from his face.

Brian stared at the glowing white skull, praying he wasn't going to throw up.

"I promised you I would get you," Matt said. "The time has come."

He moved slowly and precisely toward Brian, like a hunting cat stalking its prey.

Brian lifted the fireplace poker in self-defense—and promptly lost his balance. He fell across the threshold of the tunnel with a cry. And then everything went black.

THOSE WHO CAME BEFORE

Long after she'd stopped screaming, Alison stood staring at the skeletons. She couldn't move. She was paralyzed with terror.

"Come on, Ali." Chris took a gentle hold of her arm. "Let's get out of here."

She shook her head, still unable to get her legs to move. "I told you there was nothing alive down here," she said. "It's true! We're down here with the dead. Chris, I think we're inside some sort of tomb."

Chris gave her a little shake. "Stop talking that way. They're just bones. They won't hurt us. Now let's go!" He began to pull her away from the circle of rocks. He stopped abruptly as the strange sounds returned—the rustling of cloth, the rhythm of shuffling footsteps.

Only now the sounds were much closer than they'd been before.

Every muscle in Alison's body was trembling. She could feel the pulse in her throat racing madly. Chris was wrong. It wasn't just a bunch of bones. Something was down here with them.

A fork of lightning split the sky, this one brighter than the ones before. Alison felt Chris's hand tighten on her arm.

Gray shapes hovered around the skeletons.

In the next flash of lightning they became more defined. A woman in a long dress, like the ones they'd seen in the bedroom. A girl Alison's age, her hair swept up, her dress also belonging to the same old-fashioned era. Another girl, younger, wore her hair down with a great bow in the back. It was their dresses, Alison realized, that she'd heard rustling. There was also a man with a cigar and long sideburns, a boy Chris's age, and a teenage boy who was a little taller than Matt. All of them wore the old-fashioned clothes of bygone days.

Still holding Alison's arm, Chris began to back away. "I think we've just met the owners of the house," he said. "Or what's left of them."

The ghosts, if that's what they were, turned toward the two friends. By the next flash of lightning, the girl who was Alison's age had begun to move toward them.

"No!" Alison cried.

"Run!" Chris screamed.

Alison grasped his hand, and they began running. The darkness was treacherous. With each jagged bolt of lightning they'd suddenly see perfectly. The next second they'd plunge into an inky blackness, painfully feeling their way around sharp-edged rocks and rough boulders. Behind them they heard footsteps and the soft rustle of long skirts.

Chris cried out suddenly and released Alison's hand as he stumbled over a boulder. Alison heard him go down. And then it was as if he vanished. She couldn't see him at all.

"Chris," she called. "Where are you? *Chri-i-i-is!*" His name became a scream as she felt ice-cold bones close around her throat. She didn't need the lightning to know what was happening. The girl's skeleton was trying to strangle her.

Alison's fingers tightened around the bones that were closing on her throat. Desperately, she tried to pull them away. But the skeleton hands dug deeper and deeper.

Alison fought to breathe. The girl's grinning skull was just inches away from her own face.

Suddenly, Chris was there, pulling the bone hands from Alison's throat. Lifting the skeleton away from her, he threw it down hard. In the silent darkness Alison heard bones shattering against rock.

Chris knelt beside her. "Are you okay?"

She nodded, trying to get her breath. "Are any of the others coming after us?"

They both listened. All Alison could hear was her own harsh breathing.

"I don't hear them," Chris said at last. "At least not yet." He gestured to one of the larger boulders. "Let's sit behind that thing and take a break. You don't look like you're ready to move."

They crouched behind the rock. Alison concentrated on taking deep, slow breaths and trying to get her heartbeat and breathing back to normal. Her neck still hurt where the ghastly hands had held her. She'd never forget how cold they'd been. Or what it was like to look into the empty eye sockets of a skull.

Beside her Chris was sitting with his arms wrapped around his knees. His whole body was shaking.

"Are *you* okay?" she asked.

"Fine for someone who just wrestled with a skeleton."

"You saved my life," Alison told him. "Thank you."

Chris gave her a wry smile. "Don't be so grateful. I have a feeling the other skeletons aren't going to like it when they find out their daughter's been smashed." He stood up and held a hand out to her. "I think we'd better keep moving."

They didn't even try to figure out a direction. They just walked under the endless charcoal sky, trying to put distance between themselves and the dead.

Alison tried to think about getting back to the house. She even tried to imagine herself safe and sound in her own room. But all she kept seeing was a vision of the six skeletons lying in the circle of rocks. "What did you mean before when you said we'd met the owners of the house?" she asked Chris.

Chris ran an impatient hand through his blond hair. "I haven't put all the pieces together yet," he explained. "But we found a dining room when we were looking for you. There were six places set, and all the food was still out. As if the people had left in the middle of a meal. There were six of them and six of us."

Alison was silent, unsure of what he was getting at.

"You found clothes for a girl exactly your size," Chris

went on. "And the stuff Matt and Amber brought down for Brian was my size. Like the boy we just saw."

"How does that explain rooms that appear and disappear?" Alison asked. "Or the closet with the heartbeat?"

"I don't know," Chris admitted. "But I've been putting together some other things. Like the fact that the door was open and all the candles were lit, but the house seemed empty. Almost like someone was waiting for us. And there's also the fact that nothing in there has changed since the 1800s or so." Chris took a deep breath. "I think six people lived there then, a family. And something happened to them very suddenly. One minute they were eating dinner. The next they were gone."

"And?"

"And I'm not sure if it's their ghosts, which we just saw, or the house itself. But I feel like *something* invited us in and now won't let go. It doesn't want to let us out of the house. It wants the six of us to take their places."

"You mean living in this nightmare zone?"

Chris couldn't meet her eyes. "I mean dead."

Chapter Sixteen

THE HOUSE STRIKES BACK

Alison felt the strength go out of her at Chris's words. He was right, she realized. Someone or thing had planned this. And they were exactly where they were supposed to be. Trapped in the land of the dead. They weren't going to get out of this alive. The weird thing was that as soon as she understood that, she stopped being afraid.

She sank down against a rock. "No sense running around," she said.

"No," he agreed.

"Do we just sit here and wait to die?"

"I don't know." Chris gave her a crooked grin. "I've never done this before."

"This is getting sick," Alison said.

"Heads up!" a third voice called out.

Alison's head snapped back. She stared up in amazement at the source of the warning. Then she jerked aside as Matt's feet came crashing down right where she'd been sitting. He missed slamming into her by inches.

"Whoa!" Matt said, grinning. "Touchdown!" He stood facing her and Chris, a disbelieving look on his face as he surveyed the landscape. "What is this place?"

"Welcome to the nightmare zone," Chris replied.

For the first time in her life Alison was glad to see Matt. Around his chest was a line made from a torn, knotted sheet. It stretched up into the dark sky for about ten feet, where it promptly vanished. It *looked* like it was tied to something—but there was nothing up there. "How'd you ever find us?" she asked.

"I don't know," Matt admitted. "That's some trap door in that closet. I felt like I was falling forever. Almost like time slowed down or something." He smiled at them. "But here we are . . . wherever *here* is."

"Terrific," Chris muttered. "Now three of us are stuck."

"Stuck?" Matt said indignantly. "Do you really think I would have pulled this Tarzan routine just to be stuck with you two?" He gave them an indulgent smile. "I knew you dweebs would need help."

"You really think that rope will get us back to the house?" Alison asked doubtfully.

Matt untied it from his chest and held the end out to her. "You want to go first?"

She looked briefly at Chris, who nodded. "Go ahead. It can't hurt to try."

Grabbing the sheet-rope, Alison pulled herself up onto it. For once she was grateful that she'd had to climb ropes in gym. Using the knots for extra grip, she quickly began to climb, pulling herself up into the blackness.

As she did, the flashes of lightning grew longer and closer. They sizzled so brightly, the light was almost searing. She yelped as one bolt nearly hit the rope. But she kept climbing. All that mattered right now was getting out of the nightmare zone.

She climbed until her arms ached and her legs felt numb. She climbed until she didn't think it was possible to go any higher. Then the blackness changed, and she was suddenly in a smaller space. Reaching out with one hand, she felt floorboards beneath her. Alison blinked back tears. She'd made it back into the closet!

A crack of light came in under the door. She could see that the sheets were tied to the door knob. Then the rope seemed to dive into a pool of blackness in the middle of the floor. She jumped from the rope onto the solid floor.

"I'm up!" she yelled down into the blackness.

A moment later a knock sounded on the other side of the door. Alison heard Amber's frantic voice. "Ali? Is that you?"

"It's me, all right," Alison called back. "And I'm fine, but I can't open the door yet. Matt and Chris are still climbing up!"

"Well, tell them to hurry," Amber said. "Things out here are really bad."

Long minutes later, Chris's face poked out of the hole in the floor. Staying as close to the door as she could, Alison reached out and grabbed his hand. He clung to her as she hauled him out.

"Coming up!" Matt's voice sounded like it was miles away, but the line went taut again.

Alison stared at the floor. Was it her imagination, or was the hole getting smaller? "Hurry up, Matt!" she screamed. "It's closing up."

"Grab the rope," Chris urged her. "We've got to pull him up fast!"

She gripped it next to him, and they both started to pull on the line with all of their strength. As they pulled, the blackness grew smaller.

"Almost there," she heard Matt call. "Keep pulling."

Finally Matt's head popped into view. The hole was almost too small for him to get through. Alison and Chris pulled with every ounce of their strength.

Seconds before the hole snapped shut, Matt stumbled into the closet, shaken but unhurt.

Alison spun around and jerked open the door. Light from the corridor flooded in. She stared out at Heather and Amber's pale, frightened faces.

Amber threw her arms around Alison. "I'm so glad you're back. We've been so worried about you. And now Brian's gone."

"He's what?" Matt asked. "He can barely walk. How can he be gone?"

Heather gave them a funny look. "Actually," she said, "it's the study that's gone. The doorway turned into a solid wall, like it was never there. We've been calling Brian, but he doesn't answer."

Chris looked dazed. "What is going on in this house?"

"I don't know," Heather said. "But I think we should have listened to Matt before. It's time to get help."

"Thank you," Matt said, turning toward the staircase. "Now can we please get out of here?"

The wall to their right suddenly blurred. Like the jaws of a trap, a fresh wall slammed out, blocking off the corridor.

"I wouldn't have believed it if I hadn't seen it," Heather said softly.

Alison's eyes met Chris's. "It's what you said before. Something is trying to trap us."

"Not something," Matt snapped. "It's the house. It's cut off our path to the stairs."

THE FINAL TRAP

As Heather listened to Matt and Chris, her eyes widened in fear. Then without warning she began to scream.

"Stop it!" Alison said. "We've got enough problems right now. Don't add hysteria to the list."

"What's happening?" asked Amber. She sounded on the edge of losing it, too.

"This house is somehow alive," Matt explained.

"It's already got six skeletons down below," Chris added. "And I have a feeling it wants six more. It's doing everything it can to keep us here."

Heather shook her head. "This can't be happening," she said softly. "It's crazy. Houses aren't *alive*."

"How else do you explain disappearing doorways?" Chris asked.

"Okay, okay. We'll discuss it outside," Matt said. "Right now, the problem is to *get* outside." He stared at the wall that blocked their way. "None of you happened to see an axe anywhere, did you?"

"Don't I wish," Alison answered. "I'm in just the right mood to take this place apart, plank by plank."

"I'll settle for just getting out, thanks," Chris replied.

It was obvious that they couldn't get through the wall ahead of them. Alison glanced over her shoulder. The corridor behind them looked perfectly normal. "Maybe there's a fire exit," she suggested.

Matt shook his head. "This place is too old for that."

Chris snapped his fingers, grinning. He pointed to the sheet-rope lying outside the closet door. "But there is the balcony," he said. "We can use the rope to get down."

"Unless the house figures out what we're doing," Alison reasoned. "It may not think quite like we do, but it's got to be pretty smart."

Matt shrugged. "We don't have time to try and figure out *its* strategy." He grabbed the rope and headed for the balcony.

He never got that far. The door beside them opened with a bang. A heavy chair whizzed across the floor. Alison threw herself forward, and narrowly avoided being hit as the speeding chair smashed against the far wall.

"Uh . . . I don't think it likes our plan," Amber said.

A dresser spun out of the room, heading straight for Matt.

He vaulted over it with a yell, tossing the rope to Alison. "Get to the balcony!" he shouted. "Now!"

Alison grabbed the rope only to hear Amber scream her name. A heavy mirror had lifted itself from the wall and was flying straight toward her.

Alison hit the floor. A few feet behind her the mirror slammed into the wall, glass shattering everywhere.

Chris was beside her suddenly, his arm on her elbow. "Get up," he said. "The house just got serious with us."

Alison got to her feet, clutching the rope against her chest.

"This way!" Matt shouted. But as they tried to run, a wall about five feet away started to quiver.

"It's trying to trap us here!" Chris yelled. "Come on!" They dived forward, barely in time. A new wall exploded out of the old, sealing the corridor behind them.

"No!" Heather screamed, her voice terror-stricken. To their left, a patch of the floor was starting to waver and shift. They jumped as a wall shot up from the floor. This time, the wall hit Amber, knocking her heavily to the ground.

Alison bent over Amber, who already had a bruise forming on her cheek. She was moaning in pain. "Come on, Amber," she urged her friend. "We've got to keep moving!"

Amber shook her head and tried to stand. Instead, she wobbled a little and came down hard on her knees.

"Just what we need," Matt snapped. "Another invalid."

Alison handed him the rope. Then she grabbed Amber's arm and pulled hard. Amber barely moved. "Give me a hand," she said to Heather.

For a moment, it looked like Heather would refuse. Then she nodded tightly and took Amber's other arm. Again, they started toward the balcony.

Alison felt her hopes fade as the wall ahead of them started to shift and bubble.

"Duck!" Matt shouted as a metal standing lamp soared across the hallway. It flew over their heads, shattering the far wall in a shower of plaster and splinters.

Matt kicked in the door to their left. It was the bathroom Alison had been in earlier.

"Come on!" he yelled.

The house seemed to be getting more frantic now. Everywhere they looked walls were bubbling and buckling. Fresh boards seemed to be growing from the floor, clawing for their ankles, trying to trip them or slow them down.

They dived into the bathroom. "This doesn't lead to the balcony," Alison cried.

"Forget the balcony," Matt told her. "We'll never get there like this." He glanced around, and his eyes fastened on the one chair in the room. "Right."

He grabbed the chair, heaving it off the floor. Immediately, the chair started to come to life. The four legs began writhing like snakes, twisting around to try and grab his hands. Matt threw the chair at the window, laughing viciously as the glass exploded outward.

Chris looked around the room. "Where can we tie the rope?" he asked.

Alison's heart sank. There wasn't anything to use as an anchor! The bathtub itself had no handles or legs, and the only other thing in the room was the screen. Besides, both were part of the house and wouldn't stay inanimate for long.

"I'll hold it," Matt replied. "I'm the strongest. The rest of you get down it as fast as you can."

"What about you?" Alison asked. "You'll be trapped."

Matt gave her his cocky grin. "Not me. I'll climb down the outside wall if I have to. Come on."

Chris nodded and handed him the end of the rope. "I'll go first to steady the other end." He clambered onto the window sill and then twisted around. Grabbing the sheet-rope, he started to climb down the outside wall. Wooden slats of siding exploded outward at him, but Chris was too quick for them. Quickly he made it to the ground. He backed away from the wall, holding tight to the end of the line.

Alison suddenly realized that the storm had stopped. The ground below was a sheet of mud, but there was no rain and the wind had died down. "You next," she told Heather.

Heather nodded and started through the window.

As Heather made her way down the rope, Alison heard a sound at the door. It was like a thousand tiny feet scratching. Then the door exploded inward. She gave a cry as she saw what was making the terrifying sound.

Part of the hall carpet had torn free and was crawling across the floor toward them. Threads were quivering in the air, like the antennae of some monstrous insect.

"She's down!" Matt snapped. "Amber, you're next!"

"Definitely!" Amber agreed.

Alison stood with her back to the window as Amber snaked out onto the rope and started down. She kept her eyes on the moving carpet. Fear was churning her insides, but something was nagging her—almost as if she'd forgotten to do something.

"Hey, let's go!" Matt said, giving her a little shake. "You're the last one," he told her, panting from the strain of holding the rope. "Move it—we don't have much longer."

The last one! That was it!

"No," Alison said. "I'm not the last one! Brian's still downstairs—and he'll never get out on his own! He's going to be trapped here forever!"

THE RESCUE

Matt looked out the bathroom window, then turned back to Alison. "Everyone else is out of the house," he told her. "If we don't go now, we may never get out at all."

"I know that," she said. "But I can't leave Brian."

Matt gave her an odd look. Alison could see the indecision written all over his face. She was asking him to take a terrific risk with her. But she was determined to try and get to Brian, and she couldn't save him without Matt's help. She'd never be able to drag the crippled boy to safety on her own.

"Okay," Matt finally said. He leaned out of the window. "We're going to try and get Brian!" he yelled down at the others. "Meet us by the front door!" He didn't give them a chance to respond, but turned to Alison. "Right. Let's do it before I get smart again."

She nodded. Together they went to the door and stared out at the mad scene beyond. The floor was thrashing about wildly. The walls were shivering, and cracks were appearing in the walls as they shook and twisted.

As they started out of the bathroom, the wall that blocked the stairs shuddered and buckled. And a wide gap opened in its center.

"That's our chance!" Matt exclaimed. He dove for the opening. Alison wondered if it was a trap, if it would close while she was inside. But she knew Matt was right, and they'd never have as good a chance again. She plunged after him.

As she touched the wall she could feel the vibrations. Like a huge heart, beating slowly but regularly. She jerked her hand away, and tumbled through the gap after Matt.

He was standing perfectly still, a look of horror on his face as gazed through an open door into one of the bedrooms. "I think we have another problem," he said.

In the room a candle had somehow fallen from its candlestick onto the bed. Black smoke curled up from the pillow and a smell of burned feathers and cloth filled the air. Then the pillow exploded into flames, blowing burning feathers through the air. Alison watched in horror as the flaming feathers landed around the room. Within seconds the drapes, an upholstered chair, and a desk all began to catch fire.

There was something fascinating about the blaze. Alison stared at it, transfixed, until an urgent tug on her arm snapped her out of her reverie.

"Alison, we've got to get out of here!" Matt cried. "This way!" He sprinted for the stairs. Alison followed, hopping across the floor boards. Both of them were stumbling, working hard not to fall. Alison wished she could grab something—anything—for support. But the furniture that lined their path was shivering and snapping at them with its own bizarre life. Alison kept her hands to herself.

The heat and smoke were getting worse. Alison could hear the crackling of wood burning behind the wall to her left. Coughing, she covered her nose and mouth with her sleeve. She couldn't believe it when they finally reached the stairs. Behind her, she heard a huge crashing noise as part of a wall collapsed. The next instant, tongues of fire were licking out at them.

"The whole place is going up!" Alison screamed.

"Come on!" Matt started down the stairs, fighting to keep his balance. The steps were rattling, the floorboards twisting like snakes.

Alison struggled after him, gripping the banister for support. She let go with a scream. The banister was unwinding, and the rods that supported it bent toward them, striking at her legs.

Matt made it to the bottom of the stairs and was about to plunge down the corridor to the study when Alison heard an ominous grating noise. She glanced up and screamed a warning. Then the floorboards erupted under her, sending her tumbling painfully down the last of the stairs.

Matt rushed forward to grab her, then pulled her into a corner. Over their heads, the huge chandelier strained and groaned, then exploded.

Crystal fragments rained down around them. Seconds later they were moving again. There was the sound of another explosion somewhere behind them. Alison risked a quick look back over her shoulder. The candles from the chandelier had ignited the huge Persian carpet in the foyer. Flames danced across the entrance, casting an evil red glow over everything.

Alison suddenly realized there was a problem with her plan. How were they going to get into the study when the door was sealed? Beside her, Matt pointed to a window on the side of the house that had blown out. "We can get out there," he said, "and then break open the study windows."

Alison was the first one out the window. For a minute, she just stood there, taking in deep breaths of fresh air. Then Matt grabbed her hand, and they were racing to the side of the house where the study was.

"That's it," Alison said. "Those are the red curtains."

Matt scooped a rock from the ground and hurled it through one of the windows. Alison threw another, and then the two of them were scrambling through the jagged crack, trying not to cut themselves.

Alison stood inside the study wondering why it was so quiet. Then she realized. Though the floor and fireplace mantel were writhing, the room wasn't on fire yet. And Brian wasn't in the room!

"Brian!" Matt was shouting furiously. "Where are you? We almost killed ourselves for you! You've got to be here!"

And then Alison saw it—the bookcase that had slid out

113

from the wall and the beginning of a dark tunnel. Brian's unconscious body lay sprawled across the threshold.

Matt must have seen him at the same time, because they reached Brian at the same moment. Matt felt for Brian's pulse. "He's alive but out cold."

Alison nodded. "How are we going to get him out of here?"

Matt nodded toward the tunnel. "Maybe that's the way out."

"No," Alison said, staring into the dark passageway. She could feel the heartbeat pulsing through the stone walls. She could smell the scent of death. She knew what was down there, and it wouldn't let her escape twice.

"It's got to go somewhere," Matt pointed out.

"It leads to the nightmare zone," Alison said. "I can feel it. And I—I don't think I can go back in there."

Matt gave her a long look, then hoisted Brian over his shoulder. His face was stained black from the smoke and soot, and he looked as if he could barely stand. "The windows," he gasped. "Can you open them?"

Alison started toward the windows. Only they were gone. In their place was a solid wall.

There was no way out.

A wrenching feeling in the pit of her stomach made her glance down at the floor. The floorboards had settled back into place again. But a small blackness had appeared and was starting to grow larger. Of course the house had let them escape the tunnel. It had a more convenient gateway to its nightmare zone. It was simply going to suck them back down. . . .

Alison felt panic tearing at her like a wild animal. She looked around desperately for an escape.

"Forget it, Ali." Matt's voice was quiet. "I think we've run out of chances."

Then, far away, she heard a booming sound. Was the house collapsing from the fire? But the sounds were too ferocious and at the same time too evenly-spaced for that. She shifted away from the growing black pit in the floor.

The noise seemed to grow louder and more insistent. Then with a shattering crack, the wall blocking their escape collapsed.

Alison stared in amazement. The corridor was open now.

Somehow the three of them made it through the corridor and into the front hall. The fire ahead of them was spreading. The staircase was ablaze.

Crossing those last feet to the door meant getting dangerously close to the flaming wreckage of the chandelier.

Brian was still balanced over Matt's shoulder. Matt and Alison were both choking. Alison's skin was painfully hot. The smoke and air were burning her lungs and eyes.

Behind them, the house seemed to be going completely insane. Walls crashed, furniture shifted, and the air was filled with terrible sounds of grinding and splintering.

Finally, they reached the door. Matt grabbed for the handle and drew his hand back with a yowl. "It's red hot! I can't touch it!"

This wasn't fair, Alison thought. They were so close, and they couldn't open the door. She couldn't let the house win. She pulled the hem of her T-shirt out of the waistband of her jeans, and covered her hand with the cloth. Then she pulled open the door, and they stumbled out.

Chris, Heather, and Amber were waiting there for them. Chris and Heather took Brian from Matt's shoulders. They all waited while Matt and Alison did a lot of coughing and choking.

"Let's get out of here," Chris said, "before this entire place blows."

Together they began to make their way from the house. The light from the burning house lit up the night. Everything was illuminated, more real than ever. Alison could see individual blades of grass sticking up out of the mud. Ahead of her, Chris and Heather were supporting Brian. Amber hovered around them. Matt was still beside her. "We did it," he said, his breath ragged.

"Thanks for staying in there with me," Alison said.

Matt smiled, a shadow of his old grin. "No problem."

In front of them, behind them, the night suddenly went dark.

Matt stopped abruptly and turned around. "What the—" His voice was shaking. "Alison, look."

Alison turned and felt her knees start to shake.

"Th-there's n-no . . ." Matt began to stammer.

He didn't have to finish his sentence. She knew what he was trying to say. Behind them was a dark hill covered with a few scraggly trees. The wind carried the damp scent of earth after a rain.

"No smoke and no fire," Matt finished in disbelief.

Alison nodded, unable to believe what she was seeing. There was no house.

EPILOGUE

Three days had passed since the six friends escaped from the house. They were all gathered in Brian's living room. Brian was lying on the couch, his broken leg propped up on a huge pile of pillows.

"Can I sign your cast?" Amber asked.

Brian grinned. "I want you all to sign it."

Matt raised a skeptical eyebrow. "Even me?"

"Especially you," Brian replied. "I never would have gotten out of that house without you and Alison."

Alison looked troubled. "I talked to Mr. Clarke today," she said. "He still doesn't believe us."

Matt shrugged. "You can't blame him. I mean, he found us out there on the road. All of us were hysterical about a house with moving walls that was on fire. And then no one could actually find the house."

"He did have the police search for it," Heather pointed out. "But all they found was scrubby ground and a few trees."

Amber finished autographing Brian's cast. "The house

117

vanished," she said, as if Coach Clarke should have understood that.

"Over a hundred years ago," Chris added. "Alison and I went to the library," he said. "We did some research. Remember how Brian saw a plaque in his dream about the Campbell house?"

"But that burned down in 1864," Brian said. "The house we were in must have been built on the same spot after the fire."

Chris shook his head. "We *were* in the Campbell house. It was never rebuilt. It burned on April 25, 1864, with six members of the Campbell family in it." He gave Brian a strange look. "I think that's why you dreamed of the empty graves. They never found the bodies. I read an old obituary at the library. At the funeral service for the Campbells, they buried six empty caskets."

"This is getting creepy," Heather declared.

"It gets creepier," Alison said. "Because the Campbells and their house didn't *completely* vanish. We were in that exact same house on the anniversary of the fire. And when Chris and I were down in the nightmare zone, we saw the Campbells' skeletons and their ghosts."

"And I saw Mr. Campbell's cigar," Brian said.

"I'm confused," Amber said.

"Well," Chris admitted, "we haven't got any neat scientific explanations. But from what I can tell, the house was sort of a being of its own."

"Like a ghost?" Amber asked.

"Kind of. It's like it had a spirit or intelligence. It made itself appear for us exactly the way it was before the fire."

"And it contained all the things from its past, including the Campbells," Alison said with a shudder. "I keep dreaming about that heartbeat and the nightmare zone. I think that dark world down there was actually the heart of the house."

"It's what I thought in the wardrobe," Amber said. "We were being hunted by an alien being!"

Matt helped himself to some popcorn from a bowl on the coffee table. "That's probably the best explanation. It was never really a house at all, but some alien thing that made itself look like a house. It trapped the Campbells over a hundred years ago. I guess it needed new blood. So it was going to trap us. I mean, it did practically invite us in, with the open door and the cozy fire. And it definitely tried to keep us from leaving."

Brian fiddled with the ties on his bathrobe. "What I don't get is those fever dreams. They were so real. And the things I saw in them were real—the empty caskets, Mr. Campbell's cigar, the information on the plaque." He looked up at Matt quickly, his face reddening. "The only thing I was wrong about was you."

Matt gave one of his overly casual shrugs. "Don't sweat it. I think that house was real good at playing on people's fears. You were scared of me, and it used that. Besides, people see strange things when they're burning up with fever." He grinned at Brian. "Especially dorks like you."

Brian grinned back and threw a pillow at him.

"We'll never prove any of this," Alison said.

"I guess it's going to have to stay our secret," Chris agreed.

Matt held out his hand to Brian. "No hard feelings?"

Brian took his hand. "None."

Matt held out his hand to Amber. "Let me have that marker. This cast needs a memorable autograph."

Amber shook her head as she handed him the pen. "Still bossy and still conceited."

"You know it," Matt said. He thought a moment and then began writing in big block letters:

BRIAN—NEXT TIME YOU SEE ME IN YOUR DREAMS, REMEMBER I'M YOUR FRIEND. —MATT

Don't miss these other exciting **FOUL PLAY** titles!

HANGMAN   It looks as if there's a real hangman loose at Tiffany's slumber party.

TAG (YOU'RE DEAD)   The abandoned house next door looks empty, but when Danny and Nicole decide to play tag there, they're not alone. Someone else is there with them. Someone whose touch can kill.

SIMON SAYS   (May 1993)   Everyone always does what Simon says—when it's Simon Brewster talking. What if Simon says kill?

FOUL PLAY

When playing **HANGMAN** can really choke you . . .

When playing **TAG** has you running for your life . . .

When playing **HIDE-AND-SEEK** could get you lost forever . . .

When everyone *always* does what **SIMON SAYS** . . .

IT'S NOT JUST A GAME ANYMORE.

It's . . . **FOUL PLAY**